"You can't

"No, but I can't leave you unprotected either. And I don't mean just physically from the press. Every aspect of your life will be investigated and magnified. To the point of interrupting your work and affecting future career prospects if you choose to live separately with this baby."

"Now you're using scare tactics."

"Look at how this pregnancy looks to the outside world," he said, a thread of impatience in his words. "Unless you want to expose the whole sordid truth of how Pia and Santo asked us for our contributions while actively lying to each other, it will come out that this baby's mine. Then the speculation will start. About who you are and how you managed to trap me into domesticity. I'm known to be very circumspect with my affairs and my precious, billion-dollar sperm."

She laughed. It made her lips curve wide, her eyes sparkle and her nostrils flare, and turned her, in one blink, into a stunning, breathtaking beauty. The ridiculous thought that he had won a prize drifted through his head.

Tara Pammi can't remember a moment when she wasn't lost in a book—especially a romance, which was much more exciting than a mathematics textbook at school. Years later, Tara's wild imagination and love for the written word revealed what she really wanted to do. Now she pairs alpha males who think they know everything with strong women who knock that theory and them off their feet!

Books by Tara Pammi

Harlequin Presents

Fiancée for the Cameras
Contractually Wed
Her Twin Secret
Vows to a King
His Forgotten Wife

Billion-Dollar Fairy Tales

Marriage Bargain with Her Brazilian Boss
The Reason for His Wife's Return
An Innocent's Deal with the Devil

The Powerful Skalas Twins

Saying "I Do" to the Wrong Greek
Twins to Tame Him

Visit the Author Profile page
at Harlequin.com for more titles.

BABY BEFORE VOWS

TARA PAMMI

PRESENTS

If you purchased this book without a cover you should be aware that this book is stolen property. It was reported as "unsold and destroyed" to the publisher, and neither the author nor the publisher has received any payment for this "stripped book."

Recycling programs for this product may not exist in your area.

ISBN-13: 978-1-335-21342-6

Baby Before Vows

Copyright © 2025 by Tara Pammi

All rights reserved. No part of this book may be used or reproduced in any manner whatsoever without written permission.

Without limiting the exclusive rights of any author, contributor or the publisher of this publication, any unauthorized use of this publication to train generative artificial intelligence (AI) technologies is expressly prohibited. Harlequin also exercises their rights under Article 4(3) of the Digital Single Market Directive 2019/790 and expressly reserves this publication from the text and data mining exception.

This is a work of fiction. Names, characters, places and incidents are either the product of the author's imagination or are used fictitiously. Any resemblance to actual persons, living or dead, businesses, companies, events or locales is entirely coincidental.

For questions and comments about the quality of this book, please contact us at CustomerService@Harlequin.com.

TM and ® are trademarks of Harlequin Enterprises ULC.

Harlequin Enterprises ULC
22 Adelaide St. West, 41st Floor
Toronto, Ontario M5H 4E3, Canada
www.Harlequin.com

HarperCollins Publishers
Macken House, 39/40 Mayor Street Upper,
Dublin 1, D01 C9W8, Ireland
www.HarperCollins.com

Printed in Lithuania

BABY BEFORE VOWS

CHAPTER ONE

Renzo DiCarlo sat fuming in his tinted Maserati, watching the different occupants of the house—women of varying ages—come back from work, dates, or whatever else they got up to at the end of the day.

The two-story Victorian home, located in a village near London, wasn't where he had expected his quarry to be.

The house was sturdy and beautiful, with a redbrick facade and elegant wrought iron railings that led to a deep blue front door. Even in the waning light, he could see the vibrant garden full of flowers and neatly trimmed shrubs.

At least she had chosen a quiet little village, relatively safe, instead of a city like London or New York. He should be thankful for small mercies, Renzo supposed.

Given the excited chatter the PI he had hired to locate her had spewed about the local folklore being rich in history, he shouldn't be surprised.

Mimi Shah had always been bookish, standoffish, and more interested in documenting other people's lives. Also utterly uninterested in the public life that her world-renowned actress mother constantly courted.

That she would prefer to share a home with a bunch of working women, instead of choosing to tell his family about the child she was carrying, grated on him.

But then, everything about Mimi Shah had always grated on Renzo. Even though, in theory, she was the exact opposite of her stepsister, Pia, his sister-in-law of six years. The intensity of his own reaction to Mimi had never made sense to Renzo.

Just then, a pregnant woman stepped out of a beat-up car that had rounded the small courtyard in front of the home.

Her gait was off-balance as she bent to gather her bags, smile strained as she thanked the driver.

Renzo gripped the steering wheel tight as he watched her make her way towards the worn steps to the main door. With a hand bracing over her lower back, a cloth grocery bag in one hand, and her usual black backpack hitched on her shoulder, she took a deep breath and started the upward trek.

The way he was parked, he could see her body sketched carefully by the fading light. As if just for his benefit.

His jaw tightened.

She was slender to the point of gauntness, so her belly looked even more protruding on her thin frame. But it was her face that held his attention. All sharp angles and serious eyes, as if her stubborn nature had etched itself into her features.

Compared to her stepsister, Pia, Mimi Shah could be called average. Especially since, he realized with new insight, she made it a point to blend into the background.

Pia had been stunning—the kind of beauty that grabbed everyone's attention immediately. By the balls, he would say, thinking as a man who, for just a second, had also been caught in the trap. But that was the high point of knowing Pia.

Each minute, each day after that, the beauty would start to sag and fade under the claws of her personality. The spoiled, attention-hogging, immature woman that emerged within minutes of meeting her had forever put him off.

Pia had been vapid and shallow and manipulative and exhausting, but his brother, Santo, had loved her. Had found something in her to like.

Renzo thumped his head against the headrest of his seat, a sudden pike of grief skewering him.

How he wished Santo had never met Pia.

How he wished Santo had been stronger and asserted himself more around Pia, so she didn't play with his heart like it was a rag doll.

How he wished Santo had cut off all ties with her after the first time he'd discovered she had cheated on him.

But no...

His older brother had been as loyal and loving as only he could be. Always willing to see the good in everyone around him—whether it was his wife or their father, who fluttered around women as if he was a bee sniffing around flowers for pollen. Or Renzo himself, even when he got too cynical and ruthless for Santo's liking.

How Renzo wished he could have stopped Santo, and even Pia, from getting into the car on that stormy night and taking that dangerous curve while they were probably still in the middle of the argument he'd witnessed as they drove away.

Months later, the grief was just as fresh and just as sneaky, coming at him in a sudden blinding wave to nearly choke him. And it was one of those waves now that filled him with anger and frustration and resentment for this woman who was carrying his child.

His child...

Not Santo's. As everyone would have assumed, since she was the surrogate mother for Pia's baby.

A laugh burst through his mouth, filling the car with echoes of bitterness.

He was the father of the child that Mimi Shah was carrying—a secret only he and Santo had known. His brother had begged him to donate his sperm for their next IVF treatment, desperate to give Pia the child she wanted. Desperate to make one grand attempt at saving his marriage.

It hadn't mattered much to Renzo.

He was not a man who had ever felt particularly paternal. Maybe that came from having a father who was the epitome of selfish desires and indulgences. Or maybe because he'd carried too many responsibilities from a young age. Or perhaps, having been burned by Rosa, the girl he'd loved once, and having seen too many unbalanced relationships around him, he could never trust a woman to share his life in a way that would enrich it.

He'd happily donated his sperm because the child, whether it was carried by Pia or her stepsister, Mimi, would belong to Santo. And because a baby would bring happiness to Santo and maybe contentedness to Pia. Even his mother, he knew, had hoped for the latter.

Now Santo was gone, and Pia was gone, and her stubborn stepsister, Mimi, who had agreed to be their surrogate, was carrying his child.

Imagine his shock when the world-class fertility clinic director had reached out to him about the defaulted payments for the IVF treatment—it was just like his brother to forget people needed to be paid—and sent him all the paperwork that entailed.

He had paid for the past multiple rounds of extraction and the IVF and discovered a small discrepancy in the records.

Imagine his shock when he grilled the clinic director, exerting all his considerable influence, and discovered that his sister-in-law, Pia, hadn't even gone through the last round of extraction, but that it had been her stepsister, Mimi.

So now, Mimi, the woman he didn't like for reasons he didn't understand, and who didn't like him either, he was pretty sure, was carrying his child.

And while she hadn't known it was his and not Santo's, she had kept the pregnancy a secret for several months.

Cristo, he hated lies and manipulations and mind games. He'd had enough of them with their father and sometimes his entire family. But the fact of the matter was that whether he'd wanted a child or not, he was having one.

Soon.

And he couldn't let the status quo stand.

He got out of the car, knowing he was about to change both their lives in ways they couldn't even imagine.

But he wasn't his father. He didn't neglect his responsibilities, even if they were thrust on him by a cruel twist of fate.

This child was a DiCarlo.

Mimi Shah stared at the man standing on her doorstep, one shoulder pressed against the frame as if he expected the door to be shut in his face and was not taking any chances.

If she didn't despise drama with every cell in her and if she hadn't been prepared for him, she'd have done just that.

Renzo DiCarlo, the famous hotelier billionaire of Venice, had finally found her.

The man had always made her skin prickle—sometimes in anger and sometimes in undeniable attraction that she had managed to hide. In the six years of Pia and Santo's marriage, Renzo had always made it clear that her stepsister, their family, and Mimi were all nuisances he was putting up with for his brother's sake.

Panic uncoiled in her stomach like a snake unfurling from its nest. Perhaps that was an exaggeration aided and abetted by her wonky hormones, but not by too much.

Her hand automatically drifted to her belly, and his haughty gaze followed the gesture. It made her look defensive, she realized too late.

One thick eyebrow rose in a challenge, even as he somehow very elegantly draped himself over the doorframe without actually stepping foot inside.

Every hackle that Mimi possessed rose.

She wasn't foolish. She had imagined this very particular scenario a hundred times over the past few months. And here, she had been foolish. She had thought herself ready to face him and all that would follow.

With one mobile brow, he upended her hard-won composure and her resolve to stay calm and collected. Refusing to engage in his mind games, she moved away from the door without issuing an invitation.

His sudden laughter behind her made the small hairs

on the nape of her neck prickle. Something loose and warm trickled through her veins, like the cork had been let out of a fizzy drink.

She rubbed her belly again, this time as a comforting gesture for herself. God, the last thing she needed right now was to still be attracted to this man. It would be like kneeling in the middle of a battleground and bowing her head to the enemy.

Again, a bit exaggerated but wholly based in truth.

"This is a…cozy room, Ms. Shah." Cruel humor touched each word, along with a hefty dose of disbelief. "Nothing in the luxury repertoire of the DiCarlo hotels could match this."

"It's my home, Mr. DiCarlo," she said, matching his exaggerated sweet tone. "And no, nothing you own would make me feel as happy or as safe."

A sense of hurried alarm seized her as he surveyed the large, airy room with a leisure that grated on her nerves.

She had enough savings, from her work as a documentary maker and event videographer, to afford the biggest room in the Victorian house that one of her friends rented out. But she was also seven months pregnant, working all hours, and tired.

The room, as a result, was extremely untidy—not that she was a tidy person even on usual days. Piles of books, camera equipment, and baby bits made the room shrink to almost half. Her temporary wardrobe on a portable wheeled rack—mostly black tights and loose, colorful sweaters—took up one wall.

Boxes and boxes of baby things that she had been collecting for months—gently used clothes, toys, blankets—took up all the floor space. And then there was her knitting stuff, because it was the only way she had been able to calm her mind in the last few months, given that she couldn't even have a glass of wine.

More importantly, she had been nesting, preparing to be a mother as well as she could on her own. The realization sent a warm feeling down her spine, washing away the little flicker of embarrassment.

This was her haven, her home, where she was in control, and she felt safe. After months of fertility shots, Pia's emotional outbursts, and the mountain of lies they had been sitting on, and then the car accident and the news of her pregnancy, she had needed to be alone. While she had wholeheartedly agreed to be the surrogate for Pia, her stepsister didn't make things easy for anyone.

Had needed to find her center again after a horrible few months. Had needed respite from her mother's opinionated commentary and her stepdad John's grief. This sunny room had given her a sense of control back after months of being near Pia for the IVF treatments.

"I can see that you've been busy preparing for what's ahead."

For just a moment, she'd forgotten Mr. DiCarlo's presence. Something the man wouldn't be used to, she thought, mouth twitching.

She turned around, just in time to catch the myriad of emotions crossing his face as he peeked at the boxes. Neither did she miss the thin thread of reluctant admiration in his tone.

Leaning against the opposite wall, she managed to check him out in turn. She refused to feel even a flicker of shame about this, too.

Twenty-six, pregnant, and apparently—thanks to one of

the twisting side effects of her pregnancy—unbelievably horny. But even if she were none of those things, she could still appreciate, especially as an artist, the sheer sensual appeal of a man like Renzo DiCarlo.

Interestingly, he was the less classically handsome DiCarlo brother.

Santo had been like a marble bust with sharp cheekbones, a straight nose and thick lips. She'd just had her heart broken by someone when she met him for the first time as an art professor in one of the summer courses she'd been attending in Italy. It hadn't taken her long to realize that his perfectly boring good looks did nothing for her, though.

And soon after, Santo had turned Pia's head.

Santo and Renzo's younger brother, Massimo, had boyish good looks with twinkling eyes and a surly temperament.

But this man's appeal was something Mimi had come to appreciate only as she'd gotten older. As she'd begun to understand her own sexuality.

Renzo DiCarlo was made of imperfections—a bump in the middle of his nose, a scar through his eyebrow, a strange little dimple near his upper lip that was like a permanent indent.

As if an absent-minded sculptor, a woman surely, had gotten lost in the beauty of what she'd been creating and left a little thumbprint in his flesh.

Then there were his deep-set gray eyes and the constant dissatisfied expression that he wore. As if nothing in the world was up to his standard.

He should have been unremarkable—he had flaws enough for that—but he was more than the sum of his individual features. He had an appeal that blazed hotter than Santo's boringly perfect features ever could.

It was the air of authority and confidence he carried. And something about that air of "I can deal with anything the world throws at me" had always turned Mimi on. Even when she hadn't understood why her stepsister's new brother-in-law, who looked at them as if they were little better than garden pests, made her belly tighten and her core dampen.

She was a woman who liked to be competent in her own life, and who took matters into her own hands. Nor did she understand to this day why his confidence made her knees weak.

Maybe it was the novelty of a tall, dark, Italian billionaire being in her sphere at all. Maybe because she'd never known her own father. Her stepdad, John, like Santo, never asserted himself. Or maybe it was the age-old instinct of wanting the smartest, sexiest, strongest man around to satisfy that deep-rooted survival instinct.

Renzo DiCarlo was all of those things.

She'd stopped trying to make sense of it ages ago. It wasn't as if anything could happen between them. Then there was the fact that, within minutes of interacting with him, like now, the attraction took a back seat. The man possessed an uncanny knack for riling her up.

So she simply stood there and admired the breadth of his shoulders and how the white dress shirt neatly hugged his tapered waist, and when he went to his haunches to open the flap on the boxes of baby stuff that were everywhere, the sleek hardness of his thighs. The air inside the room was filled with his bergamot and citrus scent.

When he finished his scrutiny and turned his attention to her, it felt like a highly charged laser beam had honed in on her. Every inch of her skin came alight at his thorough, thoughtful perusal. His gaze lingered over the dark circles under her eyes—thanks to being unable to sleep well with her belly—the stress lines around her mouth that she saw deepen in the mirror every morning, the uneven flutter of her pulse at her neck, and lower.

Although mercifully, his gaze didn't linger there long.

He leaned against the wall next to the door, mirroring her stance. But while fresh tension suffused her, he looked casual with his foot propped on the wall behind him, hands tucked into the pockets of his trousers.

"Enough posturing, Mr. DiCarlo. Let's discuss why you are here."

Another rise of the damned brow, another challenge.

Mimi sighed. "I'm tired and in no mood to play the host to you."

"Let's sit down then."

"Shouldn't take that long," she said stubbornly, even though her lower back was killing her.

Anger flashed in his eyes, but when he spoke, his voice was smooth. "I'm more than happy to skip all the dramatics and jump to the Q and A session if you promise to give me truthful answers."

She bristled at his condescending tone. "I have no interest in lying to you."

"Except the giant lie of omission that we're both evading."

"I won't insult you by offering pathetic excuses. I'd do the same thing again."

"Which is exactly what?"

"Hide the fact that the last round of IVF worked and

that I'm pregnant. With...their child." Her throat prickled, but she pushed on. "Retreat from everyone I know. Escape to this quiet village. All of it."

Something glittered in his gaze. "Am I to understand that even your parents are unaware of this...development?"

"Yes. They flew to Australia right after Santo and Pia's wake for Mom's latest movie shoot."

"And may I inquire why this secrecy was necessary?"

Mimi stared at him, pleasantly surprised by the genuine curiosity in his question. She felt infinitely better knowing that she could at least read him clearly. "It was a lot toward the end. My stepsister wasn't..." She hesitated, grief and guilt scraping their claws through her.

The grief she understood. As contentious and problematic as their relationship had been, she had loved Pia. And the loss was going to change her. Had already changed her in irrevocable ways. But the guilt wasn't healthy or good for the baby, her ob-gyn had told her over and over. That Pia was gone while Mimi was alive and healthy with the child she desperately craved...it hung over her like a dark cloud whatever she tried.

"Ms. Shah?" Suddenly, Mr. DiCarlo was standing close, his large hand clutching her elbow. "You've turned alarmingly pale."

Mimi pulled away, the sudden strangely familiar scent of him filling her nostrils. She could feel herself swaying on the balls of her feet, eager to fall into his strong arms, eager to let someone else carry the weight of her burdens for one glorious moment.

"I'm fine," she said, swallowing.

With a muttered curse, he pulled back and dragged the

straight-backed chair from her desk. It thumped against the bare wooden floor as he placed it in front of her. "I won't think less of you if you sit down."

"I don't give a damn what you think about me."

"*Davvero?* Then why are you being so goddamned stubborn? You're heavily pregnant and weaving where you stand, and I'm supposed to think you're better than Pia?"

The intense frustration that colored his words, and the mention of her stepsister, sliced a little fracture in Mimi's prickly defenses. The moment she sat down, the twinges in her lower back eased, and a rough breath whistled out from between her lips.

A different kind of discomfort, something close to shame, danced in her chest. He was right. And she hated that she'd let him provoke her into acting like an immature child. When he squatted to look into her downturned face, alarm skittered through her.

The last thing she expected of Renzo DiCarlo was that he would kneel in front of anyone, much less her.

Don't let it go to your head. It's only because you're carrying the DiCarlo child, the sensible voice she trusted whispered.

"That's a miracle right in front of my eyes," she said, trying hard to dispel the mounting tension at his nearness.

"What is?"

"I didn't think the massive size of your ego would allow your knees to bend like that."

For just a fiery moment, something like sheer admiration flickered in his eyes. "I would advise you take that as a warning rather than a miracle, Ms. Shah. Trying times ahead and all that."

Mimi swallowed, both the alarm and her doubts. She wasn't going to let him wind her up with vague threats.

Pain danced freely in his gaze. His throat bobbed up and down. "I recognize the guilt in your face as well as if I were watching myself in the mirror. You're not responsible for their accident any more than I am."

Mimi nodded. Suddenly, he didn't seem like an enemy so much as another grief-stricken bystander. "Do you start to believe it at some point?"

A hollow smile curved his lips. "I'm still waiting for that day. But you..."

"Yes, I know. I have to think of the baby."

"I was going to say you were not even there that day. But I was present. I saw them leave." He rubbed a long finger over his temple. "They had been at it again, arguing like dogs. It was raining in dense sheets. I cherished the silence after they left. Until I got the call."

"I'm so sorry," she whispered, hearing the anguish in his tone.

"Me too." Then Renzo DiCarlo reached for her hands, and it took every ounce of willpower Mimi had to not jerk away like a frightened kitten in front of the big, bad wolf. "I'd like to understand why you hid the pregnancy from everyone."

"I... Pia wasn't the easiest to deal with."

"That's an understatement if I've ever heard one."

Shockingly enough, the dryness of his tone made Mimi giggle. "The last few months before the accident, it snowballed. Like you said, she and Santo were fighting regularly. But she desperately believed that the baby would miraculously fix everything. Only they were building more and more lies between them." Her breath came in a shallow gasp as she herself had skated over a dangerous lie. "At the funeral, it became too much. John and Mom and your family and you... I realized I needed to think of myself. I'd spent months being her emotional support even as I was the one going through the invasive fertility shots." The words rushed out of her. "I needed calm. Not John's heartbreaking grief. Or your arrogant commands. I...needed respite from everyone and everything, and time."

"That sounds fair."

"So glad you think so," Mimi said archly, responding to that condescending tone again.

"Ahhh...this is going to get so much harder for both of us if you react like that to everything I say."

She fought the urge to roll her eyes at him. "Then maybe don't speak in that tone to me."

"I don't know—"

"Like you're validating my choices with your agreement."

"You're a little porcupine under all that sensible softness, aren't you?"

Mimi flushed, hoping he wouldn't realize how much she liked his compliment. How much she liked that he saw her strength beneath her easy compliance. How desperate she had been all her life to be seen, especially next to her sister's brilliant beauty. That it was this man was more than alarming.

"Only one more question remaining."

Mr. DiCarlo uncoiled to his full height, one hand on his waist. He looked so deep in thought that the question came at Mimi like an arrow heading straight to her weakest point. "Why did you decide to keep the baby?"

"What?" she said inanely.

"Is it because it was Santo's?"

Hot color suffused her cheeks. "You don't know what you're saying."

"I know you nurtured a little affection for Santo. That you were the first one to meet him, the one who became his friend over that long-ago summer in Milan. Then Pia came along and stole him from you."

"And you think I kept the baby because I was in love with him?" Outrage colored her words. "So I not only was in love with my stepsister's husband but eagerly agreed to give over my body and my freedom for nine long months just to have his baby? That's a little twisted, don't you think?"

He shrugged. And even that movement was somehow elegant. "You agreed to be surrogate for a woman I know firsthand was incapable of thinking about anyone but herself, Ms. Shah. Although, it was only in the last year that I realized Pia's emotional vampirism extended to you too."

"She was my sister, and I loved her," Mimi declared, enraged.

But beneath the anger was that flicker of warmth that he had seen how exhausting Pia could be with her incessant competitiveness and petty jealousies and complex mind games. "I'm not hung up over Santo, for God's sake. Honestly, it didn't take me long to discover he wasn't my type."

"What 'type' was Santo?"

"You want me to list my dead brother-in-law's faults?"

"I just listed your sister's." His throat bobbed up and down again. "My family has already turned him into a saint, Ms. Shah. I'd rather remember the real man, flaws and all."

"Santo was irresponsible. No, that's not right. He didn't take responsibility for anything, but rather had this romantic view of life that had nothing to do with reality, and he didn't stand up for what was right. It became clear to me over the years that he and Pia lived far beyond their meager incomes, and that's all because of you. In hindsight, I think it was a miracle that their marriage lasted as long as it did."

When she looked up, Renzo DiCarlo's firm mouth was slack with shock. Mimi sighed. "I didn't mean to—"

"It seems you're a good study of character. Everything you said about Santo is completely true."

Mimi was as shocked by his honest admission as he seemed to be by hers. "Then you should acknowledge that I needed to nurture something for the man who adored my stepsister like I needed a hole in my head." She took a breath to even out her tone. "Whatever else they fought over, Pia and Santo desperately wanted this baby. They went through so much to have it. *I* went through a lot. So, no, I didn't think of not having it."

"I want to believe you."

Mimi shot to her feet. God, the man was infuriating. "If you're done insulting me, I'd like you to leave."

"We're not done."

"Fine. You're here to hash out some kind of custody arrangement, right? So can we please get to it? I've had a long day and would like a shower and dinner and my bed, in that order."

"Do you want me to order takeout for you?"

"No, I couldn't eat a morsel with you hovering over

me like some...rabid raptor, waiting to pick off leftover pieces."

He laughed, a husky sound that swathed Mimi in silky waves. "You have quite the tongue on you, *si*?"

"I'm sorry, Mr. DiCarlo, for not being as mousy and accommodating as you expected me to be."

He sighed then, and that too was distracting. Because it seemed to come wrenching out of the depths of him. It pulled her out of her own head for just a second. He had lost his brother and now had the unwanted news of that brother's child.

God, what a mess...

"I have something to tell you," he said after a long pause, "and I think you should sit down. I'd hate for you to be upset in your current condition."

"Again, it's very simple," she said through gritted teeth. "Don't tell me upsetting things."

"Remember the mountain of lies that you said Pia and Santo built between them?" Bitterness twisted his mouth. "I'd rather we don't begin this relationship buried under those ourselves."

"We don't have a relationship, Mr. DiCarlo. Neither are we going to build one." She took a deep breath. "We can arrange for visitation rights for you, if you want that. One of my housemates is a lawyer, and she assured me that I don't owe you even that. But since it's your brother's child, I—"

"It's not Santo's child. It's mine." His gray eyes held steady like flinty stones that had seen millennia pass. "Just as it's not Pia's. But yours. Wholly yours."

CHAPTER TWO

MIMI'S KNEES, IT SEEMED, were very much capable of giving out.

Mr. DiCarlo's strength and scent surrounded her as she was directed to the bed. Her breath played hide-and-seek with her lungs as his words began to sink in.

"Head between your knees," he barked like a general giving orders to his soldiers.

Mimi followed the commanding voice instinctively and bent her spine, as much as her belly would allow. Oxygen returned to her in large gulps, and she breathed it in like a gasping fish.

Although it was the warm weight of his large hands on her knees and the solid shelf of his shoulder that her forehead was resting on that became her anchor.

Two more seconds and I'll pull away, she told herself. It didn't slip her near-hysterical mind that she was finding respite in the same man who was causing her stress.

Renzo DiCarlo in her life, playing such a big role, chipping away at her armor, endangering her resolve to never depend on anyone.

It couldn't be the truth. He was lying for some twisted reason of his own. He couldn't be the father of her child, could he?

However hard she tried, she couldn't avoid the truth. Not even to stave off the moment's panic.

Renzo DiCarlo was the father of her baby.

Her baby.

Our baby, a voice said in her head, in his infuriating tone and accent. Great, now he was inside her head too.

Mimi jerked up and away from him, crawling back on the bed in a very ungainly manner until her back met the metal headboard. Looking anywhere but at him, she counted her breaths like they were teaching her in the birthing class, willing her heart rate to subside.

A glass of water appeared in her vision. She took it, gulped the entire thing down and returned it to him, hands still shaking.

"I'm sorry that I upset you," he said, sitting down by her legs. That his remorse was genuine didn't stem her confusion. Neither did that delicious scent of his.

Far too close, she wanted to scream. He was being attentive because of her condition. Not because he cared about her. God, she needed to get that tattooed on the back of her hand as a reminder to stay sane over the following months.

"Any possibility that you're in full-scale delulu-land because you've lost your brother?" she said in a small voice. Still not looking at him. "Grief does the strangest things to us."

"Believe me, Ms. Shah, if I could forget the rainy afternoon where I had to…into a cup, I would." Even his self-deprecating scoff stole through her veins like some kind of magic spell. "I checked every record at the fertility clinic. Santo told me his sperm count was too low to be of use. He found out after the first failed attempt at IVF. He begged me to keep it between ourselves, as their marriage was already shaky. I complied because I saw how much he wanted it to work for him and Pia. As usual, there was no length he wouldn't go to to give Pia what she wanted."

"And nothing you wouldn't do for your brother?"

"Santo would have been a good father. He told me Pia wouldn't even consider adoption. So yes, I agreed." Another sigh escaped him.

Mimi had the ridiculous thought that she was using up all of Renzo DiCarlo's sighs, a lifetime's quota of them.

"I'm assuming you were railroaded into a similar agreement," he said.

"She didn't...railroad me." Tears prickled behind her eyelids, and Mimi fought them back. "She cried and yelled and complained about her body being ruined by the fertility shots and how it was still failing her." Another thought struck her. "It was cruel of Santo to let her think the fault lay with her."

Mr. DiCarlo didn't jump to his brother's defense, and she liked him for it. A lot. "She begged me to help. Like you said, she wasn't an easy person to love, but I saw how the failed IVF attempts wrecked her. Anyway, I said yes to the extraction too."

"Ah, emotional manipulation was the best weapon in Pia's arsenal."

Mimi didn't deny it, even as a hot protest rose to her lips by habit. She had a feeling her state-sponsored therapist would love Renzo DiCarlo. He got her to break the pattern her therapist had been urging her to break for months now. She would not revise her complex history with Pia in her head because of the overwhelming guilt she felt.

Sighing, she looked up.

This close, the appeal of the man was a one-two punch. He was so large, so solid, so rawly masculine that she felt like she would drown in him. "Can you please give me room? I feel like I can't breathe."

Concern etched into his face, he moved down the bed, ending on a pile of washed underwear she hadn't put away yet. The sight of her maternity bras and loose granny panties made mortification rise through her in a swell.

Cursing, she grabbed them from him and shoved them behind her back.

"Are you embarrassed, Ms. Shah?" he said in a curious voice. As if he was testing something out between them.

"Annoyed by your interrogation is more like it," she said, sounding like a prickly cactus.

He didn't rise to the bait. If anything, his expression turned more serious. "I understand why you hid for all these months. But whatever anonymity you had until now will come to an end. It's a miracle the media hasn't found you out."

"Why the hell would the media care about me?"

"You're carrying a DiCarlo baby. Sooner or later, the press will find out."

"How?" she demanded.

"Because I will feature in its life, one way or the other. And because I will claim it as such." His words rang with resolve. "It's not a negligible thing. Now the whole world is going to wonder why you hid, and why I didn't welcome you and this baby into our family wholeheartedly all these months. Santo and Pia's marriage was a performative circus that dragged us all into the spotlight. Now this is like throwing fresh meat to hungry hyenas."

"First of all, the baby isn't here yet. Second of all, you're a freaking billionaire. What the hell do you care what the media says about you or your family? Aren't you all supposed be egocentric kings of your own little fiefdoms?"

"I care what our name stands for, since I built it up from scandal and ruin." Mr. DiCarlo grinned as if to take away the gravity from that. Unfortunately for Mimi, it increased his appeal a thousand times. "Are you quite this colorful in your language with everyone, or do I bring out this particular talent?"

"It's you," she said, refusing to hold back. "I'm a sensible, caring woman with everyone else in the world."

"How special that makes me feel," he said dryly.

Mimi's mouth twitched despite everything.

It was a rare sight to see Renzo DiCarlo so thoroughly put-upon, after all. When he looked at her, that tiny flicker morphed into full-blown laughter that made her chest ache and her ribs spasm painfully.

"Ouch," she said, palming her belly as the baby went into high gear and kicked.

His hands reached for her belly instinctively, and he froze so fully that it was like a watching a pouncing predator come to a deathly stillness. "Is that..." he cleared his throat, his eyes intense on hers "...the baby kicking? Is it safe? Do you need—"

"Yes, it's kicking. I laughed and must have jostled it too much," Mimi said, pulling her hands back so their fingertips didn't touch. "It's very normal. If anything,

I'd be surprised if the kicking didn't happen once every hour at least."

Hawkeyed as he was, he didn't miss her pulling away. But his large palms stayed on her belly, covering so much more ground than hers could.

A strange intimacy wove around them, and Mimi fought it with every ragged breath. Attraction to him because of some age-old instinct was one thing. But being bound to him in any way because of the baby—her entire rational being revolted against the very idea.

She wanted to tell him to remove his hands, but the words refused to form. Something about the look in his eyes forbade them.

Now she felt stupid for retreating. It felt as if she had ceded ground. Which was ridiculous because this was a baby, not a battlefield.

And moreover, Renzo DiCarlo wasn't interested in being a father any more than he was interested in tying himself to her in any way.

She needed to remember that.

It was like bubbles popping. Or like the flutter of tiny, fragile wings under his large, callused hands. Until it was a stronger tap that made his own breath punch out of his lungs.

Renzo stilled, stunned, eager to feel more of the tumbling, zapping feeling. It was unlike anything he had ever experienced. Awe filled him as the baby seemed to subside even as he waited, with a thundering heart.

Suddenly, the complete scope of what was happening in his life shone in technicolor. This was a child kicking its tiny feet or legs against its mama's belly, making itself known.

With his brother gone, this was fully his child now. *His child...*

An innocent, pure life that he was going to be responsible for, unlike the foolish, privileged, spoiled members of his family. No, that was two more lives he was responsible for now. And the second was pure and innocent too, in ways he hadn't been exposed to in a long while.

She'd been hidden by the very large shadow that her stepsister cast, and with his vision blurred by what Rosa, the girl he had loved, had done so long ago, he hadn't seen what kind of woman Mimi Shah was. And it unsettled him, as if his radar wasn't in top shape.

He looked up and met the mutinous brown gaze and nearly burst out laughing.

A strange reaction to the most bizarre encounter of his life, but there it was. He had braced himself for anger, fury, frustration that he was going to be yoked to a woman he couldn't tolerate, that he was going to be forced into a role he didn't want...

Anything but this sheer wonder at what they had created. Convoluted though their route had been.

"Can you please move your hands away? It's possible you have some rights to this child, but I'm not... I don't think we should, that is..."

He removed his hands immediately, bemused by her unusual floundering. "That is?"

"We're practically strangers."

"We've known each other for nearly six years, Ms. Shah."

And in those years, she had always pricked his curiosity, even with Pia's drama front and center. Now he brought all those little nuggets he had stored away into the spotlight.

She was a promising documentary maker. Even Pia had sung her praises. She supported herself without asking for handouts from her parents. Which was a quality he immensely respected, given all his siblings expected to be kept in luxury for the rest of their lives through his hard work. She was self-composed, and didn't date, at all.

And Pia, being Pia, had used Mimi's dating history to persuade her to be their surrogate. Santo had felt discomfited enough by the fact that he had mentioned it to Renzo.

She was as allergic to being the center of attention as he was. For some twisted reason, he had expected her, and her parents, to talk sense into Pia, to control her irrational stunts and her extravagant demands, to make her behave.

Which was nothing but stupid. He knew firsthand how hard it was to save someone who didn't want to save themselves, who believed their privilege afforded them anything they wanted. Like his father. And his sister and Massimo. And Santo, to a certain extent.

Now he pushed the intense dislike of Pia he had used as a shield against Mimi all these years aside and let the reality of their situation settle into his gut.

He was attracted to this firecracker of a woman with her bright, big eyes, sharp features and unusual but slow-dawning beauty. It was an attraction all the more dangerous and potent than any instant lust because it had snuck under his skin and stayed there, building in pitch all these years. He even liked her blunt wit and her refreshingly honest personality.

"Is there a boyfriend on the scene, Ms. Shah?" he said,

making his tone as snarky and pointed as possible to provoke her. Better to clarify everything with her up front. "What does he say to your becoming a surrogate first, and now a single mother?"

"There isn't one," she said with a vehemence he thoroughly enjoyed. "And if even there was one, I wouldn't let a man dictate what I can or can't do for my sister."

He grinned, things falling into place.

Sì, he would have considered marriage at some point.

He was only thirty-five, though, and that prospect had been relegated to the far-off future. Maybe to when he was past forty and wanted a family, when he slowed down with his luxury resort empire and his fast life. Maybe because he would have—with his genes—turned into a self-centered, indulgent old man fixated on his legacy and how far and how fast he could spread his dwindling sperm.

Instead, here was this ready-made family being offered to him on a platter.

If he could wrap his head around the idea of having this fierce, sensible, ultra-competent woman as his wife.

She was prickly, and not the sophisticated, soft society wife he had vaguely imagined when he had allowed himself to go there and would probably not agree to any proposition he made in a hundred years, just to spite him. But she was also loyal and eminently practical, and her competence aroused him more than any other woman's ever had.

Mimi Shah was perfectly tailored to be his wife and the mother of his child.

A concept he would have laughed at months ago, when Pia and Santo had been alive and well. But now...everything had changed. His entire world was upside down, and he had to adapt to it quickly. The child, unlike him and his siblings, would have a happy, secure childhood with two sensible parents.

A sudden thrill shot through him as the mere fragment of the idea consolidated into a plan in his gut in mere moments.

Her soft gasp pulled him into the present, away from his schemes. And this time, when he looked at her, he looked past her belly, if such a thing were possible.

Large brown eyes with amber flecks studied him with a discerning expression. Her silky brown hair with its golden highlights was falling away from its untidy bun on top of her head. Long lashes cast crescent shadows onto too sharp cheekbones. And then there was her mouth, small and lushly made and a lovely dusky pink.

Desire came at Renzo, soft and slow and sneaky at first, then fisting his stomach tight, flushing his insides with sudden heat.

Ms. Shah pulled back, eyes widening. "I don't trust the look in your eyes." Fingers gripping the quilt, she pulled it over her belly, as if the worn-out fabric could somehow protect her from his wicked intentions. "Whatever you're thinking, the answer's a big fat no."

Renzo laughed again. Thrice in the matter of an hour. It had to be some sort of record. *Cristo*, but the woman was sharp as a dagger, and he would have to keep his senses alert just to keep up with her.

The sheer thrill of the future unrolling in his mind made his spine tingle. At least he would never be bored with her and their life together.

"It's interesting that you read me so well, Ms. Shah. And I must say it's mutual."

"What do you mean?"

"I think there's more than all the very fair reasons you've quoted for hiding this pregnancy for so long. Especially from me."

She shook her head, although it was half-hearted.

"You knew how big Santo and I are on family, given our father is a scoundrel who thinks nothing of shaming our mother. You knew that I wouldn't let a DiCarlo child be born out of wedlock. You knew I couldn't let a child of my blood be termed a bastard by the media. You knew, and you just didn't want to face that reality." He raised his palms. "Not that I'm blaming you."

Chin tucked down, dwarfed by the quilt, she suddenly looked small and young and innocent. "If we forget whose egg and whose sperm went into the making of this baby, I would be its aunt."

"Even if it had been Santo's, with him gone, you know I would have insisted on a wedding. Deep down, you knew that. Seems you know me better than you think you do."

For a pregnant woman who had been through so much loss in recent months, she didn't buckle down and take the easy route. Even though exhaustion drew dark smudges under her eyes.

Tenderness and a fierce protectiveness danced in Renzo's stomach, provoking each other to something even more potent.

She squared her shoulders, chest rising and falling under her brown sweater. "You don't like me, and I don't like you. We've had first-row seats to an epic disaster of a marriage between people who confessed everlasting love to each other. I know you're as allergic to love as I am. There's nothing to gain by going down this path, Renzo."

His name on her lips felt like an invocation, an invitation to something new and rich. He swallowed the thick coating that desire left in his throat as his overactive mind supplied images of her breathing out his name in better scenarios. "It would work precisely because we are not Pia and Santo. Neither of us wants false promises of undying love and devotion, turning this into a daytime soap opera. Neither of us wants anything to do with love."

She didn't deny his claim, even to blindly win the argument. His admiration for her integrity increased a hundredfold. Then, suddenly, her eyes brightened. "You're well-known for your bachelor status, your fast life, your 'inability to commit to a woman for longer than a month,'" she said, quoting a tabloid article about him.

"And how would you know that?" he said silkily.

Color returned to her cheeks. "It was the one thing about you that made Pia happy. That you weren't going to bring her competition into the family for a long time. If ever."

"Circumstances change. Bachelor billionaires are toppled every day," he said, wanting to make her laugh.

Her mouth remained pursed. "You can't force me to marry you."

"No, but I can't leave you unprotected either. And I don't mean just physically from the press. Every aspect of your life will be investigated and magnified. To the point of interrupting your work and affecting future career prospects if you choose to live separately with this baby."

"Now you're using scare tactics."

"I'm not a complete bastard, Mimi," he said, frustration in his tone.

"I don't see why the media would be so interested in me and this baby. I'm a nobody. I kept my deadbeat father's name instead of taking my mom's just so I don't get caught up in her minor celebrity. Even when John asked me to take his last name, I refused. Being connected to Pia, who wanted to be a model as a teen, would have brought me attention too."

"Imagine at how this pregnancy looks to the outside world," he said, a thread of impatience in his words. "Unless you want to expose the whole sordid truth of how Pia and Santo asked us for our contributions while actively lying to each other, it will come out that this baby's mine. Then the speculation will start. About who you are and how you managed to trap me into domesticity. I'm known to be very circumspect with my affairs and my precious billion-dollar sperm."

She laughed. It made her lips curve wide, her eyes sparkle and her nostrils flare and turned her, in one blink, into a stunning, breathtaking beauty. The ridiculous thought that he had won a prize drifted through his head.

Renzo stared, his stomach clawing with sudden sensual hunger. For all that tabloid media drew a larger-than-life caricature of his romantic exploits, he hadn't rebuilt his family's finances from near debt by playing fast and loose with his time. When he did manage to have sex in the middle of his busy schedule, it was with some nameless stranger who wanted to scratch the itch temporarily like him. Nothing more.

But this hunger was different, and he wanted to give in

to it, just to know it better. He wanted to taste that laugh of hers and swallow it for his own.

"Well, if I had known it was your precious, billion-dollar sperm, I'd have made sure my eggs rejected it," she said, sighing.

He smiled.

Her gaze stuck to his mouth, another soft gasp huffing out between her lips. *Cristo*, he was thirty-five years old. How had he not known the simple, soul-searing pleasure of being the object of this woman's desire until now? Of course, he was a tall, good-looking Italian billionaire in his prime. Women did go gaga over him, but this was different.

This woman's gaze was different.

It had everything to do with who he was with her rather than what he was in the outside world. Thrilling and addictive couldn't begin to describe it. Especially for a man who'd learned the hard way that his last name was mostly a curse and only a minimal blessing at times.

"I want the best for this baby. Can I assume you do too?"

The thin thread of reluctant trust in her question made the desire clouding his head dissipate. He nodded.

"Can we also agree that being at each other's throats in a marriage that neither of us wants would not be the best for the baby?"

"Do you plan to be at my throat day in, day out, *bella*?"

"In six years, we could hardly bear to be in the same room for more than five minutes, Renzo."

"And how much of that was because of our drama-prone siblings? Do you actually remember us arguing about anything that wasn't related to them?"

Grief shone in her eyes, as sudden and painful as it had struck him earlier. "I don't want to blame them for everything that went wrong. That seems like an awful thing to do."

"And yet the reality is that we're both facing the consequences, life-altering ones at that, of choices they made, and have been conversing about it like mature adults."

"So you don't hate me then?"

"*Hate* is too strong a word for what I feel," he said, choosing his phrasing carefully.

"Let's agree, then, that we both, for some unfathomable reason, provoke the worst in each other?"

"Is it that unfathomable, though?"

The stubborn minx nodded without meeting his eyes. "You're right that I would hate to be the center of a media spectacle. Neither can I be locked in a marriage just to get the media off my back. Not even for this baby." She tapped his wrist with her fingers and then retreated, as if that was all the contact she could allow herself.

"Any woman would jump at the offer of luxury and protection that I'm offering," he said, knowing it would only provoke her temper.

Instead, she looked almost…sad. "Maybe. But I don't like to put myself in situations where I'm rendered vulnerable."

"You have a low opinion of me. What is it that you think I will do to you?" He thrust a hand through his hair, unsettled by her distrust in him. It was an alien feeling for him to have to prove himself.

"It's not that I distrust you, Renzo. It's that I have no reason to trust you. You're a powerful man who's used to getting what he wants, a man who changes partners every month. A man who will go to any lengths to do the right thing by your family, no?"

"Why is that a negative point?"

She smiled. "What if, when things go south in this supposed marriage of ours—as they inevitably will—you take this child from me? What if you push me out of its life because I didn't bend to your will?"

Anger pierced him in a sudden spike. "I have never abused my power or privilege like that in my life. I'm not my..." He swallowed the words as her eyes shone with curiosity. "We will sign an agreement that custody will be shared equally in case of separation." He studied how her quiet resolve made the amber flecks in her eyes shimmer, how even when she was tired, her skin gleamed, silky smooth. "You clearly have something in mind to make it more palatable, *si*? Spit it out."

"This marriage can happen only if you agree to a quiet divorce in, say...a year. Hopefully, the interest over Pia and Santo will die down, and the child will be legally a DiCarlo without doubt. I'll even agree to live in Italy if you still want an active role in its life."

"You think I will not?"

"A lot of things change in a year, Renzo. This way, if you wanted to back out of the marriage, there's no hassle. I'll sign a prenuptial asking for nothing at the end of the year. Except, of course, whatever you wish to contribute to the child's life. I understand you well enough to know that you'll help me financially."

Irate as her distrust in him made him, Renzo couldn't fault her for being thorough and protective of their child and its future. "How magnanimous of you, Mimi," he said, letting her name roll and writhe on his lips. "Letting me be your husband for a whole year."

"See there!" A throw pillow came at him and hit him smack in his face. "Two minutes into this discussion and you're already mocking me."

Renzo picked the pillow off his lap and made a show of fluffing it while his mind whirred. It seemed his almost-fiancée and he had way more in common than he had assumed. She needed to feel in control of her life as much as he needed to feel in control of his own. While he had accepted this about himself long ago, he understood why he had felt an instant affinity toward her and was angry life had made her feel that way too. "How old are you?" he blurted out.

"Twenty-six."

Damn it, she *was* young to be a single mother. To face the damned media and the world on her own. To face him all by herself. And yet, so far, she had acted with more maturity than even Santo had ever shown.

"So..." Another tap of her fingers at his wrist. "Do you agree?"

Feeling like a child thwarted by his favorite toy, Renzo turned his hand and trapped her fingers beneath his. "Since we're discussing terms and you mentioned divorce, should I hope that sex will be involved in this year-long agreement?"

Her pulse skittered as he moved his hold to her wrist. Her fingers were slender. The nails were painted a pretty pink, though it was chipped on two fingers.

When he glanced up, it was to find her looking like a deer caught in the big bad wolf's headlights. The tip of her tongue snuck out to lick her lower lip, and his gut tightened. "I didn't…think about that," she said, each word coming slower than the one before. "The last thing I expected today was a marriage proposal from you."

"And yet the proposal itself has nothing to do with thinking about having sex with me, *si*? After all, like you mentioned, we have known each other for six years."

Her breath roughened, and it was like sweet music to his ears. Hot color rushed to her cheeks. "You're… playing with me." Then her eyes did that widening thing that turned them into shiny pools that could reflect entire universes.

Another gasp escaped her. "You know that I'm attracted to you, don't you?"

Something about the utter mortification settling into the planes of her face both angered and softened him. *Dio mio*, they were barely engaged, and already she was turning him upside down. "It's not that much of a leap, Mimi. Most women I meet are attracted to me. It is what it is," he said with an aggrieved air.

Another pillow, another thwack to his face.

"You're the most arrogant man I've ever met," she said, half joking, half serious.

He returned the pillow to her side with what he considered to be utterly gentlemanly behavior. "Is it arrogant if I want all the facts stated and acknowledged, *bella*? You've clearly decided that I'm the villain you have to protect yourself from. Then I would have this out in the open too. Do you want me to be a loyal husband? Because it might be hard for a powerful, virile man like me to go without sex for a whole year."

"You're making it crass on purpose."

"I'm wondering if I'm allowed to seduce my very beautiful wife during the year or if that's breaking the rules she's setting for us."

Her throat moved in a hard swallow. With her eyes wide and her breath coming in short pants, she looked very young, very vulnerable. "You aren't joking."

He liked how, disbelieving as she appeared, she made it a statement. "It seems our siblings have played one last joke on us, *si*?"

"My blasted attraction to you has nothing to do with them."

"And yet, you or I would have never even acknowledged it to ourselves, no?"

"I did. Long ago. But it didn't mean I would act on it." She grinned at him, and he liked that he had finally defused the tension that had been swamping her at the idea of marriage. "But I probably have better control over my decisions than you."

"I'm counting all your allegations against me, *bella*. One day, I will take sweet revenge."

And before he did something that showed his hand too much, he pushed back to his feet. "I guess we'll see who caves in first." Soft light from the lamps kissed the strong planes of her face. "One thing I'll promise you is that I'd never hold your lust for me against you. Just a hint, though. A little begging should convince me to give in easily enough."

"When hell freezes over, DiCarlo," she shouted at his back.

Renzo threw her a grin over his shoulder and pulled out his cell phone.

It took him a half hour to make all the required phone calls. Food, security, and a doctor on call twenty-four seven, not far from the Victorian home. He hated the idea of leaving her in such advanced state, but he had no choice.

There was a lot he had to arrange and rearrange, to prepare for the baby's arrival, to prepare for his wedding. For their wedding. It had to be soon, before the news of her pregnancy broke.

"I'll be back in a week at the most. A new cell phone will be delivered within the hour along with food and..."

The silence behind him made his neck prickle.

When he turned, it was to discover that she'd fallen fast asleep. Her neck arched up, her palms on her belly, her legs crossed beneath her, she looked...intensely vulnerable.

His feet moved as if he were flying, and in two blinks, he was standing by her. Leaning over her. Feeling a desperate yearning for something he didn't understand.

He gently pushed at a stray tendril that fell over her eyes and tucked it behind her ear. But that was all he could allow himself.

This tenderness...it was because she was so young, so uncorrupted by the world, he told himself. And like any decent man would, he felt protective about her because she was carrying his child.

Nothing more.

Then, with one last look at her sleeping form, he closed the door behind him and made his way to his car.

CHAPTER THREE

When Mimi stepped off the sleek black water taxi a mere week later, she was momentarily blinded by the glint of the sun reflecting off the domed roof of Santa Maria della Salute.

She blinked rapidly, trying to process the magnificent sight before her.

No, no hallucinating here. The building in front of her clearly wasn't the understated chapel that she was supposed to meet Renzo at, but a grand, awe-inspiring basilica.

The vapid smile she'd pasted on for any passersby slid off her face. Fury filled her as a poshly dressed woman in a white shirt and black trousers approached her, a notepad in hand.

Mimi bit off the scream that wanted to escape at being thrust into the starring role of this circus. Renzo DiCarlo was…was an arrogant, egotistical, scheming bastard, and she shouldn't have trusted him at all.

But their easy discussion at her temporary residence in a village near London and the mature, sensible way he'd handled her little lie of omission, *and* their situation, had lulled her into believing him to be a trustworthy man.

So when he'd suggested on the phone—the man had

his secretary check on her three times a day along with the frequent updates he received from her bodyguard-slash-nurse—that she travel to Venice so that they could get married in a quiet civil ceremony, *so that they could hurry up and legitimize their unborn child*, she had agreed like a meek little puppet.

Naive fool that she was, Mimi had even convinced herself that being married to him wouldn't be too bad. And that it even might be nice to have a dependable partner in the early months after the baby came.

Now she was standing in front of the same crème de la crème of the Venetian society the DiCarlo family lorded over, seven months pregnant. For just a second, she wished the doctor hadn't given her the permission to travel so easily, or that Renzo hadn't been able to arrange a private jet with two medics on board.

But she was here now, and it was pointless to wish otherwise.

The white marble steps were already lined with people. Guests dressed in designer finery milled about, their conversations a symphony of accents—Italian, English, French.

Then she caught sight of the DiCarlo family—his sleek, sharp-featured sister, Chiara, and diminutive mother watching her with cool amusement, his father surveying her like a king inspecting a commoner, his brother, Massimo, looking pretty and sullen as usual, and his cousins whispering behind perfectly manicured hands.

Her heart pounded as she felt their scrutiny, their judgment. Most of which was based on Pia's behavior with them, with Santo. Which meant she was losing before she was even starting on this path.

No, she wouldn't give them the satisfaction of seeing her crack. Also, this wasn't a real marriage, and her in-laws' approval was the last thing she sought.

At the bottom of the steps, a throng of paparazzi jostled for position behind red rope, their cameras flashing like strobes as Renzo exited the taxi behind her. The air grew thick with the click of shutters and the hum of curiosity.

Mimi realized with a dawning horror that her name was already being shouted alongside Renzo's.

"Mimi, look this way!"

"Signora DiCarlo, how does it feel to bring the uncatchable bachelor Renzo DiCarlo to the altar?"

Her breath caught.

Signora DiCarlo.

They had already changed her name, and it felt as heavy as the weight of the hundred or more pairs of eyes on her. Thank the universe she had trusted her gut instinct and dressed in a loose-fitting lacy black dress.

She definitely wasn't going to spend her hard-earned money on a new dress for a wedding she didn't want.

Her bridegroom, of course, was dressed in a black Armani tuxedo that made him look like he'd just stepped off the pages of a wedding magazine.

Jet-black hair slicked back, olive skin gleaming in the sun, Renzo looked like a dream—a wet dream come true. Definitely hers, given how she'd indulged herself in the last week with images of him.

Her cheeks heated with the knowledge of what she'd done, like a neon sign painted over her face.

Reaching her, Renzo hurriedly pressed the back of his hand to her forehead. "You look...flushed." Concern drew deep grooves around his mouth. "Are you feeling unwell?"

Mimi fought the urge to slap his hand away.

But he was apparently as perceptive as he was high-handed. He tilted his head as if he needed a different point of view to consider her. "Ah...you're angry." Then he stepped close, closer than she was comfortable with, and pressed a quick kiss to her temple. The gesture discombobulated her, like everything about him did. And that scent of him sent her hormones haywire again.

"What the hell are you doing?" she whispered, her gaze lingering on his Adam's apple. Then, needing to do something with her hands, she fiddled with his straight bow tie. He bent his head, and Mimi's tummy did that roll and swoop again.

The sight of Renzo DiCarlo subjecting himself to his bride-to-be's scrutiny was the stuff of legends, and that he was playing the part so dutifully with her was enough to make even her sensible head go dizzy.

"Did you know that you have a very open face, Mimi? You telegraph everything you think, every emotion that moves through you, in your eyes. The last thing we need is to give the press more fodder about us."

"I'm the one giving them more fodder?" she hissed under her breath. His scent was seriously messing with her composure. "You promised me a quiet civil ceremony. This...is hardly that. And how powerful and influential do you have to be to reserve this place in a matter of one week?" She didn't give him a chance to reply to her rhetorical question. "You didn't even have the decency to tell me ahead of time. Do you realize how humiliating I find this? All these people staring at me, judging me, wondering which trash pile you pulled me out of…"

She didn't understand why tears pricked behind her eyes. Usually, she didn't give a rat's ass about how she was perceived by anybody. But something about this situation made all her hackles rise.

Renzo frowned. "You can hardly blame me for this after the stunt your mother pulled in the last week."

"What?" Mimi blinked, her frown as genuine as her bafflement. "My mom's in Australia."

He took her hands in his, and again, she had to fight the urge to jerk away like a scared kitten. He was doing it for the press. She could hear the *click-click* of cameras.

"Did you talk with your mother in the last week?"

Mimi pressed a hand to her brow. A slow dawning of what could have happened made her words stutter. "Yes. She…she surprised me with a video call. It was one of those times when she remembers that she's my mother. I didn't think before I picked up—I was tired. I forgot to hide my belly. I'd been preparing all week to tell her about it. But she saw it, and the whole thing exploded. In the end, I had to calm her down."

Renzo's fingers moved from her palms to her wrists, stroking and soothing her fluttering pulse. "What did you tell her?"

"Not much." Mimi tried to think back to the call. "She went off on how I lied to her and didn't think of how this would affect her. Wouldn't let me get a word in… I think all I said was that you and I are dealing with it. That's it."

He looked up, her frustration mirrored in his gaze.

A groan escaped her as she suddenly realized how her

very dramatic mother might have construed that sentence. "Oh God. What did she do?"

"It's fine. I'm dealing with it, and it's not your fault."

"Please…just tell me. There's a reason my mother and Pia got along so well. She's always been under this impression that I have no good sense when it comes to men. And even at the best of times, her protectiveness of me is performative."

"She issued a statement to some local tabloid that the DiCarlo men have a history of mistreating her daughters—starting with Santo, of course, and now me. I don't know if she said it in those exact words, but the gist of her statement was that I got you pregnant and discarded you because that's what my family does with women."

The granite-tight set of his jaw said how much he abhorred being tarred with the same brush as his father. And Mimi knew, from all the gossip Pia had shared about Santo and his family, that Renzo was meticulous about keeping his love life and his business affairs utterly private. Only after he'd left had she realized how much her comment about him using his power to separate her from the child would have hurt him.

It had been a defense mechanism on her part, that claim. Because one-on-one, the attraction between them had been too much to handle. As had been his shocking marriage proposal. In her heart of hearts, she knew Renzo DiCarlo would never use his power to hurt her or anyone.

For God's sake, the man was marrying her to stop being called the same names as his philandering father. Even though he owed her nothing, even though the media croaked regularly that he was a confirmed bachelor. "What a mess," Mimi said, horrified by how her mother had, in the end, messed it up for her.

"Of course, someone here picked up her statement. I told you—they're constantly looking to revive Pia and Santo's tragic love story, as they've begun to call it. This smoke was exactly what they needed."

Mimi closed her eyes and took a few deep breaths. "Right. So you decided to do damage control by throwing a wedding in front of the basilica and inviting half of Venice."

"I had to," Renzo said in clipped tones. "I can't have anyone thinking I discarded you. Honestly, this is not a bad idea. Now the entire world can think this is a regular conception and that I'm not ashamed of either you or this baby." He regarded her curiously. "Isn't this better than all the speculation about who you are and why I hid you away for so long?"

"No, this isn't better. Nothing is worse than me standing here, seven months pregnant, walking toward you in front of all these people in a mockery of what a real wedding should be."

His hands moved to her shoulders, and he pulled her close. "I called you last night. You didn't take my calls. You just kept texting me that everything was fine and you would show up."

"I was out with my friends, and then I came back early because I..." Mimi swallowed the small bite of the truth. If she told him that she'd been feeling uneasy all day yesterday and today, God knew what he'd do. "I was tired, and I'd had enough of your high-handed instructions. Honestly, I wanted one last quiet night before all this drama. Now it looks like my circus radar was justifiably going haywire."

"It's not as bad as you think. You have that glow about you, and your…" He stepped back as if to get a better view of her and laughed as he fully took in her black dress. "Ahhh… I get it now. Last little rebellion."

Despite the twisting in her stomach, Mimi smiled. How was it that he was the one man who saw her inner motivations so clearly? And that the fact that he could see her always made her smile?

"If you care about how you're perceived in all this, I can have the wedding attendant put you in a designer dress in two minutes, and then you don't have to be embarrassed."

"No. There's no way I'm pandering to these guests who don't even know me, the stupid media, or you. I'm getting married in this dress. Take it or leave it."

If she thought she would darken his mood with her stubbornness, Mimi was proved wrong.

Renzo's grin only deepened, and he gave her a short bow, as if she were a queen making the most solemn declaration for him to execute.

"There's one more thing we need to discuss," he murmured.

Groaning again, Mimi muttered, "Jesus, Renzo. At least take pity on the fact that I'm two months away from giving birth. What else is in store for me?"

"When I tried to get in touch with your mother, I got John instead. I told him of my plans, and he insisted on being here for you today."

Her heart scuttled into her throat as Mimi searched the crowd for the tall, lean figure of her stepdad. That tight clutch of tears returned to her throat as if it had never left. "John's here?"

Renzo nodded, his sweep of her features intense. His knuckles danced over her wrist in soothing strokes, as if he knew the mention of her stepdad would push her that much closer to the edge. "I told him that it was up to you whether you want to see him here today. I know you haven't seen him since the wake, and I understand how hard this might be for you."

The depth of his perception when it came to her emotions…it took her breath away anew. And the warmth it enticed in her belly scared her.

Mimi pressed her forehead into his chest, uncaring that she was messing up his pristine suit. Or that he could mistake it for her softening toward him. In that moment, she needed his support to stay standing.

Not a surprise that John would offer to be here for her. To give her away, in what was nothing but a farce, because he wouldn't want her to be alone. Even though he knew now that she was having the baby that was supposed to be his daughter's, though he'd never shown any preference between her and Pia.

He had loved them both the same from the moment her mother had married him. And Mimi had tried for his sake, more than anything, to be a good sister to Pia, who, like her, had never known her other parent, having lost her mother in childbirth.

That cunning sneak grief came at her again, making her tremble on the warm day. With Renzo's arms around her shoulders now, she wasn't alone with it.

"Shh…*cara*. You don't have to see him if you don't want to," Renzo whispered.

Mimi wrapped her arms around his waist loosely, pretending for one moment that this was real. That his care for her was real.

"Does he know how this pregnancy came about? Did you tell him that the baby's…ours?" she asked, for once hoping he had taken control of the situation. She didn't have it in her to go through it with her stepdad, didn't have it in her today to be strong for him.

"Yes, I told him the entire twisted story, and it will stay with him. I want the world to know that this is our child. I don't want any confusion—now or later. I loved my brother, but this is our life now. And there's no need to feel any guilt for making the best of the cards we've been dealt."

"It's not that simple for me," she muttered.

"What about this bothers you?" Something about the way he asked that question, his voice low and threaded with a hint of genuine concern, made Mimi unravel a little more. If she wasn't careful, he was going to turn her into a home-trained little puppy who did whatever he wanted every time he spoke in that husky tone.

"I don't like this much public scrutiny. And then there's the fact that I'm at a disadvantage here, Renzo. This whole wedding circus makes it look like I trapped you. You're known for your bachelor status—for enjoying your freedom, for enjoying the fast life. Now it looks like you have no choice but to marry me because I'm cooking your bun in my oven. All my life…"

She swallowed the words that wanted to rush out after that. No need to bare her entire vulnerability to his eyes.

"All your life what?" he demanded.

She shrugged, not meeting his eyes. Not willing to set aside her concern to simply soothe him.

Even though his frustrated grunt urged her to do just that.

"Then how about we do something that shows the media and everybody else here that you're not trapping me into anything? That I'm standing here because I want to be here."

She looked up at him, and her breath left her in a rush at the glint in his eyes. Whatever it was, Mimi knew she was going to hate and love it at the same time. "Like what?" she said, making it clear that she didn't trust him.

Renzo's grin turned wicked. His hand moved to her waist, pulling her closer in a way that made her hyperaware of every camera trained on them. And somehow, he even managed to shift a little to the side so that he didn't nudge up against her belly. And then he clasped her jaw in a firm grip. "Something like this."

Mimi stared, transfixed, as he dipped his head and touched his lips to hers.

His were cool and soft while hers were burning hot with a longing she couldn't push down. She'd have thought it impossible for her body to even register any more stimuli...but she was minutely aware of the puffs of his breaths against her lips, the indents of his fingers against the nape of her neck, and the low rumble his chest made under her own fingers when she rubbed her lips lazily against his...and then there was the way he draped himself over her, with those broad shoulders shading her from the entire world, as if the moment was too private to be shared...

And then even that level of awareness fell away, and she was spun into pure golden sensation as the kiss deepened.

"Open, *bella*. Let me taste you."

The sensual shock of his words made her gasp, and he took immediate advantage, swiping his tongue inside her with a mastery that made her groan. On and on he kissed her, in long sips and little nips and lazy bites, stealing every inch of air from her lungs and every ounce of sense from her head.

Mimi sank into the kiss, lazy heat unspooling through her, unraveling her. And when he turned the soft nip into a sharp pull of her lower lip, dampness filled her panties, and she lost the little balance she had.

She fell into him, and he steadied her, but not before her belly brushed his…erection. A lash of pure primal heat held her captive.

God, to be wanted by this man was unlike anything she'd ever known.

His low curse feathered over her skin as his lips drifted down her jaw. Large hands rounded her shoulders gently, belying the heat and intensity of the kiss. "I only meant to give them a little glimpse into this. Now it won't look like I'm being dragged to the altar against my will."

"How very sacrificial *and* performative of you, Renzo," she said, something she couldn't control creeping into her tone.

Surprise made his mouth slacken while his gaze searched hers. Whatever he saw there, he sighed. Not that it stopped him from rubbing his thumb pad against her lower lip. "You're a hard negotiator, *cara*."

She swiped the back of her hand across her lips as if to

erase the kiss, though the heat of it lingered stubbornly, mocking her. "I didn't ask you for anything."

"And yet I want to admit that only point one percent of that was for the press. The rest was for me. For us." He frowned, as if he didn't like the taste of that word on his lips. *Us*...a feeling Mimi completely understood. "I simply wanted to test a theory."

"What are the results?" she said, her voice sharp enough to cut glass.

"That we could have an altogether entertaining marriage if we so wished," Renzo replied smoothly, his wicked grin unwavering.

Mimi's fingers curled into fists at her sides. "You're unbelievable. One blistering kiss and an unplanned baby does not guarantee marital bliss. And please, warn me next time so that I can prepare myself appropriately for the performance. Although I should tell you, the acting gene missed me."

"If I told you I was going to kiss you senseless, then you'd have put your defenses up and ruined the spontaneity. That would hardly convince anyone, don't you think?"

"I would still like to be included in the plan, please."

Renzo chuckled, the sound infuriatingly rich and self-assured. "That's a fair ask. Next time, I'll tell you how much I want to kiss the hell out of you." His gaze moved to her belly. "Like you, I don't like surprises, and we've had enough to last a lifetime."

"We never agreed on the sexual side of this arrangement," she huffed in meager protest.

"*Sì*, but I'm a patient man, and the chase is half the fun."

"You're not chasing me," she sputtered, the very idea making her body hum.

"Of course not. I'm talking about you chasing me, sliding one rung down at a time from your high-and-mighty ladder. Begging me to give you what you need."

Empty air huffed out through her lips as Mimi wondered at the sheer audacious ego of the man. "I'll never beg you for kisses or sex, not if you were the last man on earth. In case I didn't make it clear earlier, you're not the man I'd have chosen to have a child with."

His smile dimmed, replaced by something unreadable. And Mimi had the most ridiculous notion that she had grazed the impenetrable arrogance and confidence that he wore like a second skin. But then the walls were back up, and he was the smooth, charming Renzo DiCarlo again. "I promise to not crow when you lose, *bella*. Should be easy since I will be too deep inside you to care about winning. Your surrender will be the true reward."

Before she could respond, he turned on his heel, his stride confident as ever as he walked away, leaving her standing there, fuming.

And Mimi swore to herself that she wouldn't surrender to the arrogant Italian, even though the vow felt just a little hollow beneath the lingering heat he had provoked in her body.

CHAPTER FOUR

Mimi stood by the window in the vestry, staring at the light as it fractured across her dress. Her hands twisted nervously at the fabric, the silence in the room feeling heavier with each passing second.

The space was small and plain, in contrast to the magnificent architecture of the grand cathedral. Soft wooden pews lined the walls, a narrow stained-glass window casting muted hues of red and gold across the floor.

Despite her resolve to not soften towards her confounding bridegroom, she found herself utterly grateful to him. He had given her the quiet retreat she desperately needed, tucked away from the bustling preparations outside.

Both to catch her breath and to have a private chat with her stepdad.

The door creaked open, and Mimi turned, her chest heavy with emotion.

John stood there, his tough face etched with fatigue and concern. Usually a simple man, he looked out of place in his designer suit, and yet he was here. He'd traveled thousands of miles just so she wouldn't be alone.

"You look beautiful, Mimi," he said gruffly.

Mimi's eyes filled up, probably turning her into a raccoon, but she didn't care. "I'm... I don't know what to say.

I didn't expect you to want to be here. After the last few months…" Her words choked and died in her throat, her stepsister's name refusing to come to her lips.

He stepped inside, letting the door click shut behind him. "You think I wouldn't be here for your big day?"

Her hands automatically went to her belly as she blinked the tears back. "I did this for her, John. This was supposed to be her baby. And it all fell apart."

He closed the distance between them and took her hands in his, his own eyes filling with tears. "Of course you did this for her. You were a good sister to her, Mimi. Never doubt that, okay?" His grief slashed lines through his face. "She made it so hard some days to love her, but we loved her. And she knew that, Mimi. She knew how much she was loved. So we'll remember that, yeah?"

Mimi nodded, his words chipping away at the grief and guilt, making her burden lighter. On an impulse, she threw her arms around his solid form, feeling like that little girl who had gazed up at him in wonder the day her mother had married him, and he had told her that they were a family now. "Thank you for coming. I can't tell you how much your words mean to me. How much I struggled these past few months."

He patted her back awkwardly, shocked no doubt by her sudden display of physical affection.

She'd never been one to show it. Pia's warning on the day of their parents' wedding, that he was her dad and not Mimi's, had killed any inclination to do so.

"None of that now, Mimi. You hear me? Not in your condition." He pulled back. Feeling self-conscious, Mimi released him. "Your mother wanted to be here too."

She nodded, not putting much stock in her mother's wishes.

John cast a look around as if he was searching for eavesdroppers, then leaned closer. "Everything really alright, love? You sure about this? Renzo—he's…" He stopped himself, his words faltering. "He's always struck me as a solid fellow, more reliable than Santo, at least. But marriage is a big thing."

"A solid fellow?" Mimi said in disbelief. "He's…far too arrogant and has always looked down on our family."

"Yes, but then, his gaze was colored on his brother's behalf, no? Pia didn't make it easy for anyone, and Santo enabled her, and…it's good that Renzo's stepped up to look after you and the baby after how you both got here."

"I can look after myself," she said perversely.

John's smile was like a rainbow in a cloudy sky. "Of course you can, Mimigirl. You've always had a sensible head on your shoulders, but sometimes it's nice not to be alone. Nice not to go through life all by yourself."

"Is that why you married Mom?" Mimi had no idea where that question came from. "Because you were lonely?"

John looked stunned and then shook his head. "No, I married your mom because I love her, Mimi. I know it might not look like that, the way she carries on and orders me around, but your mother…she cares, in her own way."

"I'll take your word for it, John," Mimi said, out of all pretense.

"Say what you need to, Mimi," he said, shocking her. "Get it out of your system. All this beating around the bush didn't help Pia one bit, did it? Believe it or not, your mother's cut up that you didn't tell her about the pregnancy."

Mimi stared at the resolve in his eyes. "You want me to talk about why I've never felt the remotest connection with the woman who raised me?"

John blanched but nodded. Apparently, the day's shocks would keep coming. "You know, I've never held it against her that she sent me off to boarding school or that she prioritized her career over being a mother. That she brought me home only after she and you married. But she...she never tried to connect with me on any level, John. And yet with Pia..."

"Easier with Pia because they cared about the same things, no? Clothes and acting and all the silly, superficial stuff. Your mother can't handle anything deep. You, Mimi, are the most self-composed, intellectual, thoughtful woman I know. I wouldn't be surprised if your mom didn't know what to do with you."

"That's an easy excuse," she said, even as shock tumbled through her. Then there was the fact that when it came to Renzo, all that composure went out the window.

"Why do you think she caused such a big ruckus when she found out you were pregnant?" John said softly. "She wanted to be here so badly, but I discouraged her. I didn't want her to make things more awkward for you and Mr. DiCarlo."

"It only complicated matters for me," she said morosely.

John's shoulders slumped, and for a moment, he just stood there, beaten down. Finally, he said, "She wants to make it up to you, Mimi. And believe me, it's never too late for that. Never too late for admitting that we are wrong. I'm so sorry, love."

"What do you mean?"

"I know Pia made things hard for you. Until a few years ago, I didn't see it, Mimi. I didn't realize how insecure my daughter was and how you became the target for that."

"It's fine. It's all in the past."

"It's not fine, and it's not in the past when the hurt she caused you is still…there." He rubbed his palms over his eyes. "I see now how alone you must have felt. What with your mom's head in her own career. I should've stepped in more. I should've done better by both you and Pia."

"You were there for her when she needed you most," Mimi said quietly. "And now you're here for me. That's what matters."

"You did always have the best heart out of all of us, darling." His hand lifted, hesitating for a moment before resting on her head. "I understand why you didn't tell your mama or me. But we're here now. We can help you raise the baby. I don't want you to make choices because you think you have to. This marriage, is it what you want?"

The question made her heart stutter. "It's not a love match, but it's what is necessary right now."

John studied her for a long moment, then sighed. "Alright, then. But remember, you always have a home with me and your mother. We love you, Mimigirl." He held out his arm. "Now, will you please give me the honor of walking you down the aisle?"

Tears prickled at the corners of her eyes as she looped her hand through his arm. "Thank you, John. For coming, for…everything."

He patted her hand, his rough palm warm against hers. "Always, love. Let's get you married, then."

Together, they turned to the door, the quiet solace of the vestry giving way to the bright, extravagant facade her immediate future seemed to demand.

Mimi hated to admit it, even to herself, but Renzo had been right again.

No one, not even the couture-dressed guests with their brilliant diamond chokers and beautifully cut features, could question his commitment to this union, this baby, to her.

Inside the basilica was even more overwhelming than its exterior.

Gilded domes soared high above, adorned with intricate mosaics that seemed to shimmer with an otherworldly light. Marble columns lined the nave, their veins catching the flicker of countless candles.

Rows of chairs filled with impeccably dressed guests fanned out before the altar. The space hummed with a different kind of energy now, the chatter quieter but no less intense.

The air was heavy with the scent of incense and beautiful white roses alluringly draped over every possible surface and the whispers of the gathered elite of Venice.

At her appearance, no doubt.

Mimi took a deep breath and straightened her spine, clutching John's arm as they began their slow walk down the aisle. Each step seemed to amplify that pulsing twinge in her lower back, but she decided to ignore it for now. No wonder her body was making up new cues in concert with her agitated, anxious mind.

But the ache, along with the weight of her seven-month pregnancy pressing down on her body, was a constant reminder that this wasn't a fairy tale. As much as Renzi DiCarlo had fabricated it just so.

And then, like a fish taking bait, she caught his gaze.

Renzo, so impossibly handsome that she still thought she might be dreaming, stood with a confidence that seemed to anchor the opulent surroundings, that seemed to mock her own misgivings about this wedding.

He had more to lose than she did by tying himself like this, didn't he? His freedom as a bachelor, his fast life. He hadn't even sent her the prenup agreement she'd insisted on.

Did he trust her that much? Or was his wealth so vast that whatever cunning scheme Mimi might run later didn't worry him?

The grandeur of the basilica dimmed in comparison to the sheer intensity of his gaze. He wasn't looking at the gilded arches or the sea of society's finest but at her. The echoes of the kiss they had shared glimmered in his eyes.

Her chest tightened and she forced herself to focus on each step she was taking toward him. The marble beneath her feet gleamed under the soft light, the polished surface cool through her thin shoes.

Soon, she was there and suddenly, she felt trapped. Her breath felt equally so in her chest, making her dizzy.

Renzo's expression softened immediately, his hand reaching out to clasp hers with a tenderness that made her breath come easy. It was maddening how quickly that look calmed her.

John pressed a soft kiss to her temple and, with one

glance at Renzo that made him nod, released her into his care.

"You're almost there, *cara*," Renzo whispered as she moved to his side. Immediately, the already familiar scent and heat of his body enfolded her as if in a gentle embrace.

And for a fleeting moment, the grand trappings of her surroundings fell away. There was no high society, no fairy-tale wedding. Maybe not even her large bump.

There was only Renzo, and the remembered heat of their kiss, and the terrifyingly audacious hope that maybe there could be more than just the baby to bind them.

The water taxi pulled to a stop in front of the Grand Rialto DiCarlo, the pride of Renzo's empire. Renzo stepped out first, nodding at the concierge who scrambled to open the door for Mimi.

His gaze swept the crowd that had gathered along the cordoned-off street, their cameras flashing like strobe lights.

The spectacle grated on his nerves. More on Mimi's behalf than his own. He'd grown up surrounded by luxury and paparazzi. Every inch of his life had been under their greedy scrutiny.

He knew personally what it was to be judged as a DiCarlo first, and barely as himself. Whereas his new wife…hated that kind of spectacle and had been protected from her mother's fame at the boarding school.

His wife… Renzo frowned at the stirring of excitement at the phrase.

Dio mio, it was one thing to accept fate and adapt accordingly, and a whole other to pant after his wife, who showed no such inclination toward him.

He extended a hand to Mimi, helping her out of the boat. Her face was pale, her posture stiff. The exhaustion of the day and the strain of carrying their child were etched into every line of her body.

Guilt pressed down on him like a heavy anvil hanging around his chest. He could have made this day easier for her, but his vanity about people's perception of him had gotten the better of him. Was he any better than his father then, if his self-worth needed validating?

"I can show my face at the reception for a half hour. Is that good enough?" she said, his little trooper.

"No. To hell with the reception and the guests. I'll take you straight up to our suite. You should rest," he said, leaning closer to her so his voice wouldn't carry.

"Are you sure? I don't want you to say I didn't hold up my end of the bargain later."

"*Cristo, cara.* I'm not the devil. I can see your exhaustion clear in your face."

She glanced at him, her lips pressed tightly together as if she wanted to argue but couldn't muster the energy. "Okay. Can I ask you for a favor, though?"

"What?"

"In an hour, could you send someone to check on me?" When he frowned, she colored. "Just as a precaution."

"Half an hour and I'll come up myself. Let me get rid of everyone."

He thought she would refuse his offer, but she gave a meek nod.

Every inch of him went on high alert. For Mimi to agree to any proposal of his without a protest was not normal in any way.

Without another word, he placed a hand at the small

of her back and guided her through the lobby, ignoring the curious stares of the staff and the opulence he usually took pride in.

The elevator doors slid open with a soft chime, and Renzo stepped in, pulling Mimi gently along. She winced as she stepped inside, her hand brushing the curve of her belly.

Renzo's brows knitted. "What's wrong, *bella*?"

Before he could finish, she stumbled, clutching his arm. Her weight nearly toppled him, and his hands shot out to steady her. "Are you alright?" he demanded, his voice sharp with worry.

She didn't answer immediately, her face contorted in pain. And then, a sound he didn't expect—a faint splash against the polished floor.

Renzo looked down, his mind blanking for a fraction of a second as he registered the darkened leather of his shoes and the small puddle spreading outward.

Mimi's breath hitched, her wide eyes lifting to meet his. "Oh God," she whispered, panic lacing her voice. "My water...broke."

The words hit him like a punch. His heart thundered in his chest as he took in her stricken expression. "What does that mean?" he demanded, even as his insides shook at the implication. He'd demanded and received a crash course in pregnancy and baby delivery from his mother mere hours ago. Water breaking meant...the baby was coming.

"It's too early, Renzo," she said, her voice trembling. Pale and small, she looked incredibly fragile. "The baby— it's not due for two more months. If it comes now..." Horror painted itself across her features in greedy strokes.

His insides swooped with fear, but he beat it back.

"Shh...*bella*," he interrupted, his hands framing her face. "Look at me."

Her eyes were glossy with unshed tears, but she obeyed, her breath coming in shallow gasps.

"We'll handle this," he said firmly, his voice steady even as fear clawed at him. "Everything's going to be fine, Mimi. I'll be there every step of the way with you, and I won't let anything happen to you. Okay? Just breathe, *cara*."

She nodded, her fingers gripping his lapel as if it were the only thing keeping her upright. "You're here with me, and you'll make it right," she chanted, her eyes already far away.

Renzo's heart steadied at the naked conviction in her words. He reached for the emergency button in the elevator, his other arm wrapping around her protectively.

The grandeur of the hotel, the cameras outside, even the weight of the day—it all faded into insignificance. All that mattered was getting her to safety and ensuring their child came into the world as it should.

And keeping his wife's faith in him intact...because suddenly, it had become the most important thing in the world.

CHAPTER FIVE

THE NEXT TWENTY-FOUR hours were the worst of Renzo's life.

All of his arrogance—that he could control his destiny, that he was the lord and master of his fate—crumbled into so many pieces under the weight of his new wife's panic.

They had rushed to the hospital, where the world-class obstetrician confirmed her fears—the baby was coming early, and it might not be able to breathe on its own.

Words had been choking in his throat as they checked her vitals and helped her slip out of the ghastly dress that had drained all the color from her face. Although a few minutes later, he changed his mind about the wedding gown. The pale white hospital gown made her look washed out, reducing her to a shadow of worry and stripping away all the attitude and toughness that defined Mimi.

"I... I've been having these twinges in my lower back, you know, for the last two days," she said, her voice trembling. "Which is why I came back early from my girls' night out. They've been there for a while now. I guess I didn't notice that they were gathering momentum. They did hurt, and I should've told you, and I should've gone to the hospital, but I didn't think much of it, and I..."

Her fingers dug into his chest, trembling, and Renzo wished he could take even a fraction of her pain away.

"What if I neglected all the signs my body was giving me? What if I rushed to the hospital two days ago and—" Her voice cracked, the words dying on her lips.

It was the moment Renzo felt the weakest in his entire life. His wealth, his influence, his intelligence—none of it could help him now. All he had were his words, his faith, and the enormous admiration he felt for this woman.

This woman who never let herself weaken in front of anyone needed his strength now.

"Stop, *bella*," he said, gathering her to him. He made his tone as stern as possible to get through the panic, to help her find the steady ground she needed right then. "You cannot blame yourself, Mimi. The specialist has assured me that this happens sometimes for no good reason. Everything was fine at the last checkup. Only the baby seems to have shifted now. Nothing you did, nothing you thought, contributed to this. Do you hear me? If anybody is to blame, let me take it upon myself then."

Her tearstained eyes widened as his words turned into a rough growl. "What if all this is because of the stress I caused you? Because I convinced you to marry me, and then I surprised you with this giant farce of a wedding?"

"No," she interrupted, shaking her head, fair to the last. "This started way before this morning," she said, her voice exhausted, drained of all fight.

Renzo dismissed the attendants, the physician, the nurse—everyone. Then he lifted her, settling her in his lap. "Listen to me, and listen well, Mimi. You did nothing wrong."

He placed his palms over her belly, willing their baby

to understand his words as well as its mother. In the matter of mere hours, his entire perspective had been turned upside down. "This baby could have been the unluckiest, losing the parents that wanted it so much before it even came into the world."

He tipped her chin up and wiped at another rogue tear from her soft cheek. "Do you know what convinced me to marry you?"

"Your obsessive need to play controlling hero in my life?" she said, a sliver of her irreverence coming back into her eyes.

Cazzo, if they got through his together, there was so much more to look forward to. Not a single day with this woman would be boring. But neither would she chase excitement or fame or sacrifice everyone else's happiness around her just to indulge her own whims.

"The faith, the strength, and the sheer joy I saw in your eyes when you talked about how much you already loved this innocent life. Such clarity of purpose in one so young…"

"Keep talking, Renzo. I believe I'm beginning to see why the media adores you so much," she said, hiding her face in his throat. But he heard the wobble there. And it tore at him that he couldn't fix everything for her.

"You didn't care that you hadn't planned for this baby, that it came out of a twisted set of circumstances. You simply remembered how much this baby was wanted by Pia and Santo—and so you would want it and love it." He blew out a choked breath. "I surprised myself when I proposed marriage to you. Did you know I don't even eat breakfast without planning and optimizing it?" These were not words he'd ever thought he would utter, but they came easily now.

"I don't know what to say," Mimi whispered against his neck.

"After losing Santo, your faith made me believe too. Gave me a purpose again, a way to honor his wishes even though he's gone. You got this far, Mimi. Now I want you to calm down and let things unfold, okay? The stress you're feeling now—the guilt you're putting on yourself—cannot be doing you or the baby any good."

Her cold hands cupped his cheeks, and he realized with a start that this was the first time she'd touched him willingly. It felt like a milestone in an avalanche of them rushing at him. "Thank you for making me listen," she whispered. "If something—"

He silenced her with a kiss, knowing they needed something more than words. A deeper connection. *Cristo*, he needed her taste and her faith in this moment as much as she needed his. The soft press of her lips against his jolted through him.

She tasted of tears and toothpaste and pain, but Renzo refused to let her go. Suddenly the idea of a world without Mimi in it, without this baby in it, felt like a nightmare he couldn't imagine.

Slowly, she relaxed in his arms, and he continued to stroke his hands down her back. Her breasts pressed into his chest. Her softness engulfed him.

It was only the awful situation that they were in that had her cuddling into him like a kitten, but he enjoyed it just the same. Whatever this woman chose to give would be a prize, he told himself, his thoughts fragmented by her nearness.

Like the flutter of butterfly wings, her lips moved under his, and she began to kiss him back. Softly, tentatively, as if afraid to shatter the fragile peace of the moment.

He opened his mouth to capture her every huff and groan. Fingers twisting in his chest, she clung to him as if he were her only lifeline.

Heated desire filled him, but more primal, more urgent than anything he'd ever known. As if every cell in his body understood the raw poignancy of the moment, as if desire could be more than just his body's need.

With a rough groan, he plundered her mouth, seeking more faith, more strength, more warmth. As if her own need for validation in this hard moment mirrored his, Mimi matched him stroke to stroke, fervor to fervor, until breathing itself became secondary. They lost themselves in the deep, drugging kiss for long moments, worries and the outside world shut away.

She pulled back and stared at him, pink mouth trembling. "Thank you for today, Renzo. I…couldn't have coped without you."

"No need to thank me for doing my duty, *bella*," he said, knowing how much it cost her to say that. He pressed his forehead to hers, his voice a gentle murmur. "We're going to be okay. You, me and the baby."

Then came the long process of labor, which had lasted several hours. She was the one in pain, and yet Renzo thought he might climb the walls of the clinic in his worried frenzy.

Finally, after what felt like ten eternities to him, his son had been delivered, though they took him away immediately. All he'd gotten was a passing glimpse of him since Mimi had lost consciousness and they had been trying to revive her. He thought his soul might have cracked a bit at the sight of her bloodless face. And yet, next to the horror was the wonder, as if both emotions could exist side by side.

A baby boy, his heart kept shouting at ear-splitting volume, as if it meant to wake up him from the numb stupor he had descended into.

A son who was months early and needed help with breathing. And his wife, his brave, fragile wife, was buried deep under the effects of anesthesia.

Did he want to see the baby? the specialist had asked him. But Renzo had refused—not that he wasn't dying to see the tiny life that had come into the world despite all the odds stacked against him. The baby Santo would have loved more than life itself, like he had always loved Renzo. The baby Pia had wanted with a desperation he'd never seen in her.

The baby he already loved more than he could have ever imagined.

But he wanted to see him with Mimi by his side. He wanted to savor this new, raw, incredible experience with her, together. *With his new wife...*

It was a foolish, sentimental thought, that rational voice he usually nurtured reminded him in its usual mocking tone.

But he ignored it.

Legs kicked out, Renzo was slouching in the plush chaise lounge as Mimi stirred awake in the oversized bed, the faint rustle of her breathing uneven at first. He tugged at his tie hanging loosely around his neck, a nervous gesture he usually had under control.

The vulnerability painted across her features made him shoot to his feet a little unsteadily. Worried about when she might wake up, he hadn't moved or slept a wink, and his eyes felt gritty.

"Renzo?" she said in a dry voice.

He switched the small lamp on at a low setting and poured water from a jug.

Face pale, with faint gray shadows beneath her eyes that made sharp blades of her cheekbones, Mimi looked drawn and waxy. Her usually shiny dark hair was matted and damp around her temples.

A grimace crossed her face as she pushed up on the bed. "The baby?" she said, clamping her fingers on his wrist.

Something twisted in his gut, making him feel as if an invisible line had been crossed. No, he'd been dragged across it by fate, and now there was no going back. Only forward.

He was a husband and a father. Two things he'd never thought he'd be. Two things the men in his family were abysmal at being.

"Renzo?" Mimi whispered, though her tone rose in pitch.

He sat down on the bed next to her and handed her the glass. "He's doing as well as possible," he said.

She shook her head, stubborn to the last. "Tell me. Is the baby…" She swallowed audibly, and tears ran down her cheeks.

Out of the depths of numbness, fresh anger coursed through him, and he welcomed it. Anything was better than the black void of waiting he'd been drowning in for hours.

"Enough, *bella*. I will not have you sick again. Enough tears. Drink the water, and maybe I will tell you."

She bristled, exhausted as she was. "You're mean. Deep down, I always knew that." But she took the glass from him and guzzled down nearly half of it.

It spilled around her mouth and down her neck. Which, in turn, made her gasp.

Renzo grabbed a napkin and wiped away the excess. Her pulse fluttered weakly under his fingers, the bones of her clavicle jutting painfully.

She grasped his wrist, her fingers ice-cold on his skin. He fought the urge to nuzzle deeper into her touch. "Please, tell me."

"We have a son, Mimi," he said, the words pushing past the chokehold in his throat. "He's healthy, although they tell me he cannot breathe by himself because he was early, like you said. Everything else is pretty good. They have to keep him in the neonatal unit for the next few weeks. Once his stats improve, we will take him home. You and I will take our son home."

Fresh tears filled her eyes, but she blinked them back. A small, precious smile fought through the tears, curving her lips. "A son..." Her smile bloomed deeper, sending color to her cheeks. Her chest rose and fell with her shallow breaths. The same awe he had felt danced in her eyes. "What does he look like?"

"Right now? Like an oversized, wrinkled grape with a thin layer of fluff on his body."

Just as he had intended, she gasped, burst out laughing and then smacked him. "Watch how you speak about my son."

"Our son, *bella*," he corrected her softly, though the emotion behind it was intense and overwhelming.

Possessiveness he had never known swamped him, fisting his insides. Without an outlet, it made him as angry as a bull.

Growing up, he'd watched his father dally and flirt and conduct scandalous affairs with one woman after the other, neglecting their mother, neglecting his children, neglecting the hotel chain his grandfather had handed him on a platter.

Making their family a target for tabloid press and fortune-hunting women. Not that he had any doubts about some of the women's claims about their father.

Self-preservation then had been the only armor he had had left.

He hadn't let anyone close—not Santo, not his sister, Chiara, and definitely not their mother, who had always been close to breaking. Hadn't let anyone see how hurt and isolated he felt even surrounded by all of them.

Worse, as soon as he'd reached eighteen, he had to become their protector. Including their father, to curtail his behavior, to save him from his own excesses. Their mother, from completely shattering. Because no one else was going to. He had worked hundred-hour weeks with his grandfather's help, guiding the company back into profits, building it bigger and better in the last few years with new branding and acquisitions.

Power, he had realized, was the only way to control his father, the only way to exist outside of weaknesses, one's own or others'.

He had tailored his life to never want anything from anyone, whether it be kindness or help or even affection. The women he'd dated had known that and had called him a ruthless, heartless monster. But he hadn't felt anything more.

And yet now, this woman and their child seemed to have razed all his armor to dust. Making him feel all sorts of emotions that he didn't know how to process, or how to exist with.

"Our son," Mimi said clearly, her gaze holding his, conveying something he couldn't put into words.

Renzo wondered if they would develop their own language now that they shared this magnificent tiny life. Like his grandparents did.

"Please tell me more about him," she said, tugging fretfully at the IV tube.

Renzo leaned forward, letting some of his weight drop onto her legs. The small intimacy immediately filled her cheeks with a burst of color. "He has a full head of jet-black hair and the DiCarlo nose."

Her lips turned down at the corners. "He looks nothing like me?"

"He has your ferocity and your strength, *bella*. They told me premature babies like him struggle with their sucking reflex, and he does too. But when they get him to clamp on the bottle, he's fierce at drinking it up. They said it's a great thing that he has such a good appetite."

Fresh tears rolled down her cheeks, and she swiped at them with the back of her hand. "More, please."

He chuckled and took her hand in his, the naked hunger in her eyes calling to something in him.

He wanted her to look at him with such bare desire,

wanted her to depend on him for everything. There was something extremely arousing, extremely motivating about winning the regard and respect of a strong woman like her. A woman whose strength of character shone like a diamond's facet.

Merda, but only he could turn winning his wife over into a challenge for himself. But there it was, a sparkling new goal. One that set his entire being on fire.

"What else, Renzo?" she demanded, tugging at his fingers.

She had long fingers with chewed-up nails and chipped nail polish. The strangeness of her hand in his gave Renzo whiplash for a second. They had been through a life-altering event together, but she was still pretty much a stranger who didn't believe in his commitment.

The uncertainty of it prickled against his skin, demanding action. Demanding he arrange his future, *their future*, to his satisfaction. He never doubted his decisions, but everything they had gone through in the past few days had only hardened his resolve that Mimi and their son belonged with him. Permanently. His little family would operate on mutual respect and fidelity and their love for their precious son.

No, it was just a case of figuring out what she wanted and giving it to her.

He patted her hand and let go. The very vivid visual of this strong, beautiful woman surrendering everything to him was enough to keep him going.

"Renzo? What's wrong?"

"I'm wondering if I should tell you a little truth. It doesn't paint me in a good light."

"Are you having second thoughts about being a father?"

Alarm danced in her eyes, but she rallied fast enough. As if she were used to dealing with disappointments from others. The very thought stoked his ire. "Doesn't matter. A child's birth is such a big event in one's life that it's normal to doubt yourself. I'm okay if you want to annul the whole thing…"

"*Merda, cara!* You really think very little of me, don't you?"

The vehemence of his curse made her blanch, but she didn't back away from him. "Commitments like these are hard for certain people. I don't want to trap you."

"Noted," he said, half growling the word at her.

She leaned forward and rested her forehead on his shoulder. "I… I would be crushed if you walked away now. And not just because you're a powerful, arrogant billionaire who can arrange the world just so for me right now."

He laughed, his breath hitching at the soft graze of her body against his. How could this fragile woman be so strong? "Flattery will get you everything."

"Tell me, please. I don't want secrets between us when it comes to…*him*. Or how we feel about this whole parenthood thing. Like you said, we're doing the best we can, and there's no script for this. No right or wrong way to feel."

"I haven't seen him yet," he admitted, a hundred emotions coursing through him. But none that he could hold on to. He felt like he was constantly caught up in a river current, barely staying afloat. "Everything I told you, I was simply repeating what Massimo told me."

"Why didn't you see him, Renzo?"

He kept his eyes averted from her, not wanting to telegraph something he didn't have under control. "You were unconscious, and it felt unfair that I see him first when you were the one who carried him all these months and cared for him. So I asked Massimo to tell me. He seems excited that he's not the baby of the family anymore."

She tugged his chin up, and the smile blooming on her face was...so brilliant that it should have blinded him. "Shall we go now and see our son?"

He laughed and drew her closer. As if they had gone through the same ritual a thousand times, she tucked her head under his chin and wrapped her arms around his waist.

Renzo felt the desperate need to kiss her again. To taste her sweetness and her desire and *her*...just one more time.

He beat back the urge. Their relationship was supposed to be built on trust and mutual respect, not his hunger for her. Yes, he was attracted to her, and that would only make their marriage pleasant. Maybe become part of their foundation too. But he couldn't become a slave to his own needs and mess this all up. He couldn't let anything but rationality rule his head.

"*Sì*, we should. But the nurses will have to check you first. They worried that your blood pressure was too low earlier. You fainted when they tried to get you to sit up to go to the bathroom."

She turned her face up to him and scrunched her nose. "Please tell me I didn't embarrass myself."

He sifted his fingers through her tangled hair. A soft groan escaped her chapped lips, sinking deep into his flesh. "Even if you had, it's okay." Tenderness engulfed him. "Did you have a name for him in mind?"

She tensed immediately, and he stroked his palm down

her back. The need to soothe away every ache from her—whether it was of body or mind or heart—engulfed him.

He had always been the one to take charge of his family affairs, even though Santo had been older. From ordering their father to control his unending flings to making sure their sister married the man she loved, to taking charge of their dying hotel conglomerate and growing it to the billion-dollar luxury resort empire it was today...he had taken control of all of it.

Not once had he bemoaned the duties that fell to him.

Then why should this overwhelming need to relieve his new wife's burden be anything different? Especially since he'd already decided that this marriage would be as real as he could make it between them. She was under his protection, and his patterns were far too deep-rooted to deny them now.

"It's your call, Mimi. Whatever you decide, I'm okay with it."

He felt her shuddering exhale, her slender body swaying in his arms. Her words were a muffled whisper against his chest. "They wanted to call him Luca if it was a boy. It was one of the few things they immediately agreed on."

He tightened his arms around her, grief twisting his stomach. This day would have been so different if Santo and Pia had been alive. And yet he couldn't imagine a different reality.

Did it make him a selfish bastard that he didn't want to?

"You like it?" he said, clearing his throat. There was no point in letting the ghosts of the past dictate their lives now.

"I do," she said simply.

"Luca it is then," he said.

She burrowed deeper into him, chanting their son's name over and over again.

CHAPTER SIX

Mimi hated the idea of leaving the close-by hotel when Luca had to stay in the hospital.

Her suite at a nearby DiCarlo hotel, which was a two-minute walk, was close to paradise.

But it was nearly a month since Luca had been born. The team of doctors had assured Renzo that her own medical needs had been stabilized and that she should continue recuperating in a *more restful and comfortable environment.*

Although she thought it was Renzo who wanted her in a more comfortable environment.

Because her new husband was an arrogant, high-handed billionaire who thought he knew the best for her, he'd deemed that Mimi would leave the nearby hotel and move into his penthouse. And hadn't seen fit to inform her until the last minute.

She had thought they were going for a quick boat ride.

Instead, it was only as the sleek wooden motorboat eased toward the dock that Renzo deigned to inform her she was leaving the hotel.

Trapped in the awe-inspiring sight ahead of her—the building was a striking blend of modern luxury and Venetian tradition with its smooth sandstone facade gleaming in the setting sun—she had stared open-mouthed. It was close to the Grand Canal but far removed from its touristy chaos.

The soft slap of water against the dock mingled with the distant hum of gondoliers' songs and the occasional clatter of footsteps on cobblestones. The air carried a blend of salt from the lagoon, the faint metallic tang of the boat's engine, and the floral sweetness wafting from planters lining the building's private landing.

It annoyed her that he was making her decisions for her, and yet there was too much to take in. Especially after being ensconced amid the cloying sterility of the hospital and the hotel for a month.

The staggering luxury of his home only increased her discomfort as they rode the private elevator to the penthouse. When the doors opened, she got lost in the view once again.

The city stretched out before her through floor-to-ceiling windows, a breathtaking mix of shimmering water, Gothic architecture, and the golden glow of streetlights reflected on the canals.

Renzo dropped her little overnight bag on the sleek coffee table, his tall frame at ease in the starkly modern surroundings. "Welcome to your new home, *bella*," he said calmly, holding his hand out to her. "I would carry you over the threshold, but I think you're not in the mood."

So he knows that I am angry?

Mimi stared at his hand with its long fingers and square nails. As familiar as her own. The memory of how gently and carefully those large hands could hold their son tugged at her heartstrings even now.

The sight of their tiny son cradled against his broad

chest was fast turning into her favorite thing in the world. For some foolish reason that wasn't based in reality, she had assumed that Renzo would falter at holding such a fragile newborn or that, like some of her friends' partners, he would balk at being a hands-on father.

But nothing was off-limits in his role as an attentive, first-time father, and if possible, her ovaries had melted at how easily he slipped into the role. The idea of building a true connection to him and nurturing their new family for real had seeded deep inside her heart, despite her struggles to keep herself outside the fake dream she was living in.

As a husband, though…she didn't know what to expect from him.

She knew that he had been rocked to his core that Luca had been born early and that there were complications with his birth. But all along, he'd been there for her, every step of the way, every hour.

In the last few days, however, he had retreated.

The smushing hugs and the quick kisses at her temple and the wrapping his arm around her…he had touched her less and less. And the realization that she missed it hit her smack in the face.

Was it because she wasn't a near-hysterical, needy woman anymore? How could she be angry that he was making decisions for her and yet want him to hold her as if she were precious for as long as possible?

He'd also been gone more and more, work diverting his attention from her and even Luca.

It was exactly what she had prepared for, what she had known would happen, and yet it left her restless, distressed even. Ridiculous because this was real life, and he owed her nothing more than what he'd already given her.

"I know you're angry with me, *cara*." Renzo's voice gentled as if he were dealing with a wounded animal that might take a bite out of his hand any moment. He moved to stand by the windows, watching her with those sharp, assessing eyes. "But you're so exhausted that you're weaving where you stand. Won't you come in?"

She didn't miss that he had modified the command into a request. Feeling like a recalcitrant child, Mimi walked in, her footsteps barely audible on the polished wood floors.

The living room was a study in understated luxury—sleek Italian furniture, a low glass coffee table, and abstract art that somehow complemented the ancient city spread out below them. A wide terrace wrapped around the penthouse, with glimpses of the glittering lagoon visible even from inside.

Exhausted wasn't the right word for the feeling in her body. She felt…empty. Hollow. Her chest ached with grief she couldn't explain.

"I've arranged for everything you might need," he said, gesturing subtly around the penthouse. "There's a chef on call who will deliver freshly made meals four times a day. A nurse if you feel unwell, a lactation specialist to help you pump. And then there's the housekeeper, though she won't disturb you unless you call for her. There's also a nutritionist, a mobility coach, and—"

"Are you that desperate for me to get back into shape?" she said, infuriated by his directions. The effort he'd gone to should have comforted her. Yet the clinical perfection of it all—the penthouse, the arrangements, the instructions—only deepened the sense of isolation. "Am I to transform myself into the perfect trophy wife suitable for the name DiCarlo?"

"That's the most ridiculous thing I've ever heard," he said, nostrils flaring. "The doctors recommended that you would spring back better if you incorporate light exercise and stretching. I wanted you to have an expert so that you don't hurt yourself. As for turning you into something you're not…"

"I don't want your bloody experts, Renzo," she snapped. Did he have to remind her that she'd never fit into this sophisticated life? And why the hell did that hurt so much? "Take me back. You had no right to bring me here without consulting me."

He moved closer, tension radiating from him. And for a reason she couldn't fathom, Mimi ate up the tension. She liked that he was at least discomfited by all this. God, was she turning into a drama queen like her mother and Pia? Why did she feel this unnerving urge to shatter his self-composure?

"I tried to bring it up," Renzo said. "You refused to discuss it."

"Because I want to stay back at the hotel where I'm close to him." Her voice broke on a catch, her breath coming in harsh pants. Every inch of her ached, her muscles felt heavy, and yet nothing could touch the monumental void in her chest. She knew she was clinging to her infant son and yet, suddenly, it felt like there was no place for her anywhere else.

"I don't want to be here." She covered the few steps between them, thrusting herself into his space with a belligerence she'd never displayed with anyone in her life.

"Or was the hotel bill becoming too much for you?" It sounded ridiculous to even her own ears.

His sigh, more than anything, made a spark of shame flicker in her chest. "You will not provoke me tonight, *bella*." He lifted his hand to her face, seemed to think better of it, and pulled away. "It isn't good for you anymore at the hospital, Mimi. The nurses told me you were constantly obsessed with his stats. They said you raised the alarm a few times because you were worried that his breathing might have changed. You even wander over there in the middle of the night."

A prickling heat behind her eyes made the vision of him shimmer. God, she was so tired of crying. How could her tear ducts make more of them? "So they were spying on me for you?"

His hands clasped her upper arms, his grip firm and yet somehow gentle. Tight lines fanned out from his eyes and his mouth. The shimmering vision solidified, the deep trenches exhaustion had carved into his face becoming clearer.

While she'd been obsessing over Luca, Renzo had been working long days and nights, only stopping to spend time with her and Luca. And not for one moment had he shown even a glimpse of impatience or tiredness. His strength, both mental and physical, seemed to be relentless. The small spark of shame in her chest burned brighter.

"No, *bella*. They are worried about your mental health, as am I. Luca will come home one of these days, and I'm sure you want to be recovered and well for him, *sì*? Staying there isn't helping you, Mimi."

"What if something happens to him while I'm gone?

While I'm sitting here in the lap of luxury sipping some disgusting green juice?"

Renzo tilted his head, his brows drawing together. "That's only your fear speaking. You said yourself how much you trusted the neonatal specialist."

"I will go mad here, Renzo. I can't—"

"Give me three days and nights, *cara*." The tips of his fingers pressed against her clavicle on both sides. And the touch, more than his words, pulled her from the edge of hysteria. "If you can't bear it, I'll take you back. And in the meantime, we will visit him three times a day. *If* I am assured that you're eating and sleeping properly."

His offer surprised her and for just a second, she could think outside the worry constantly clouding her thoughts. And he had so many more people to worry about than just her and their son.

The realization snapped her out of the deep abyss she'd been dwelling in for days now.

She had never in her life, not even for a moment, become a burden or the source of worry for anyone. Not her mother, not John and not even Pia. If anything, she had gone out of her way to be self-sufficient, wary of trusting anyone enough to show her doubts or worries.

And yet with Renzo, she had been behaving miserably. As if he were her enemy instead of her partner, while all along, his patience and strength had been constant.

She'd forgotten how hard it was for her to lean on someone. For some reason, Renzo made it extra hard. She wanted to hide away all her vulnerabilities. She wanted to never lose his respect, never let him see the yearning to belong somewhere.

The yearning to belong to him, which had only gotten stronger in the last couple of weeks.

Some of it was her hormones riding her hard, but some of it grew because she'd had a taste of what it would be like to be utterly his. To be the center of his laser-eyed focus, to be able to lean on him, to know him like no one else did.

She nodded, not raising her gaze above his throat. "That's fair," she said softly. "I'll go unpack."

Which was an inane excuse, because she had nothing to unpack. But she needed to get away from him and his painfully perceptive gaze. Needed to find her balance.

She walked past him toward the hallway he'd gestured to, her bare feet silent on the cool floor. Without noting any details of the bedroom, she went straight to the closet. Of course, it was the size of an entire flat.

She undressed quickly and pulled on a silk robe hanging in the closet.

It dwarfed her, but she didn't care. All she wanted was a bath and then sleep, so that she could shake off this dark mood and wake up refreshed to see Luca.

Feeling much better already, she strode to the en suite bathroom and stilled.

Stunning as the rest of the penthouse, it was a marble paradise with a rainfall shower and a freestanding tub that seemed to belong in a spa.

Renzo was kneeling by the tub, his fingers dipped into the steaming water. In his other hand, he held tiny glass bottles that he was perusing intently.

Pulled up tight, his black trousers highlighted the wiry strength of his thigh muscles. The same strength her own body was beginning to not only recognize but crave melting into.

Mimi looked away, only to find her attention snagged by his profile. A sharp, too-long nose, a high forehead, and a mouth that could have been shaped by any one of the art geniuses from this part of the world...he was too magnificent to look at, too larger-than-life to be real.

Marriage had always been firmly in the No column for her in the near future. Especially after Pia had played with her emotions. When with Pia around, she always doubted a man's attention toward her. The two boyfriends she'd had had been more excited about her connections to Pia than about her.

And yet...this man was her husband. A "duty" he took very seriously. The title and their bond seemed as irrevocable as the changes in her body, mind and soul that giving birth to their son had wrought.

And she couldn't deny that for all his high-handedness, there was a rough kindness hidden beneath the arrogance. A loyal heart and a sensible head that made up the thrumming power of his personality.

The exact kind of man she'd have eventually wanted in a partner, *if* she wanted to go that route. Nor did she fool herself that it was his physicality that tugged at her every time she looked at him. All the female nurses and staff, while extremely professional, hadn't missed the easy sensuality he wore like a second skin. A couple of them had teased her, even congratulated her for "landing and leashing" such a man.

And yet had anyone—man or woman—seen him like she did? Gotten glimpses of who he truly was beneath the designer suits and the luxury CEO mantle? Seen the flashes of overwhelming love in his eyes as he looked at their son, a responsibility he had never foreseen?

Now, with the rising steam making enticing curls of the short locks of his hair, cuffs pushed back to reveal corded forearms, he looked...touchable, real. As if he existed on the same plane as her.

Mimi fisted her hands by her side, fighting the urge to sink her hands into that thick hair. She wanted to touch every strong plane and hollow divot he was made of, muss up his perfection, somehow reduce him to the same level of distraction as he did her. Some of it was sexual, and some of it sprouted somewhere else that she was far too scared to examine.

"What are you doing?" she said, to fracture her own fascination.

He turned. A small smile tugged at his lips, deepening that misplaced dimple. "Drawing you a bath. Do you prefer lavender oil or rose?"

Mimi fiddled with the knot of her robe, suddenly aware of the deep V at her chest. "I can do that myself."

"I don't doubt that, *cara*," he said, before upending the tiny bottle into the bath. Instantly, the room filled with a cloud of scented steam. "Rose it is. I think I smelled it on your skin before." His voice turned into a gravelly whisper. "It suits you well."

Tendrils of warmth uncoiled through her lower belly. The sensation was so sharp, so different from the aches and pains that accompanied childbirth, that she gasped.

"Come, check if the water feels right," Renzo said, still kneeling on the floor, the cuffs of his white dress shirt damp. His olive skin glowed with the sheen of the steam.

She reached the tub and hesitated, her body feeling

altogether alien. Which was saying something after the last month.

His gaze traveled up, lingering when the robe parted to reveal a good amount of her bare thigh. Awareness sparked through her, a tiny, flickering pulse.

She had pumped before leaving the hospital, but already, her breasts ached with heaviness and milk. But there was more, too—a pleasurable ache, as if her body was determined to remind her that she was a woman who had her own needs, that she was more than just a mother.

Still, she felt self-conscious outside the familiar surroundings of the hospital, without their son as the bridge. The fog of the last few weeks lifted suddenly. She felt like she had been dropped in the middle of some unknown land with a stranger who affected her in ways she didn't understand. And yet he wasn't a stranger either.

She rubbed her chest, confusion welling up over all the things she wanted from him.

Renzo's throat moved as his gaze climbed higher. It snagged for an extra moment over her lips before colliding with her eyes. "You have that look again, *bella*." Distaste colored his tone.

"Like what?"

"Like I'm your enemy. Like I am the big bad wolf who might swallow you up."

"I don't consider you my enemy. But I…" she fiddled with the knot at her waist "…have been making you the target of my…frustrations and fears. And that's unfair. I'm sorry."

Surprise made his chin dip, and a smile played with the corners of his lips, though he didn't let it show. "Your honesty, as always, astounds me."

"As for the second," she said, his gaze making her bold, "I'm aware that you could very well be the big bad wolf, Renzo. And that you might swallow me up if I'm not careful." *Physically, yes, but in other ways too*, she didn't say.

He laughed and it sent a million tingles through her nerve endings. Mimi stared open-mouthed at the sheer beauty the smile carved into his face.

His chest was still shaking when he said, "Do you plan to hide yourself away?"

She shook her head, slowly bending toward the lip of the tub. "The ideal scenario would be to swallow you up in return. Since I have no idea how to do that to a man like you, the next best thing is to enjoy the inevitable, I guess. Which, with your enormous experience, is what you've been saying, I imagine."

He held her gaze and touched her hand. "A man like me, hmm. Am I so different from other men you've known, then?"

Mimi stared at him, aware of the pulsing tension his casual question carried within. But she couldn't quite put her finger on the source. "Of course you are. And not just because you're wealthy or powerful or look like that."

"What is it?"

She shrugged, unwilling to lay everything out for him. The fact was that he was unlike any man she'd ever met or dated, and he made her feel things she'd thought she would never feel.

"I keep thinking I know you now, *cara*," he said, a bite of disgruntlement to his tone, "and then you go and surprise me all over again."

"I just want to make it through the next year without ending up at each other's throats, Renzo. Whatever else happens in the meantime..." She shrugged, unable to put it into words.

A line tied his brows, but he said nothing more.

She swallowed, bent low and checked the water. It was hot but just right. Before she could move back, he pulled her hand underwater.

Mimi squealed with surprise, then laughter as he let go and splashed her. She half fell into his lap and retorted with her full might. Within seconds, his face and neck and chest were drenched.

Laughter burst up from her chest, breaking through the tightness of grief and ache, making her shake. She continued her onslaught, wetting them both thoroughly in the process.

With an exaggerated sigh, he wiped his face with one hand, while his other arm rested right under her breasts, pressing into her with the perfect amount of pressure. God, how she adored being held by him like this, like she was precious to him. Like he couldn't go another minute without having her up against him.

Like she wasn't just his son's mother.

His cheek pressed into hers as he tucked his chin onto her shoulder. "It is good to hear you laugh, *bella*."

She nodded, refusing to look into those penetrating eyes.

Slowly, he hefted her until her butt was resting on the lip of the tub, and he waited until she had her balance.

Once he was sure, he got up and moved around the bathroom, pulling out his shaving kit and shedding his damp shirt.

Mimi watched the smooth planes of his muscled back without blinking, those tendrils of warmth encasing her again. His chest was lean and sculpted with a smattering of wiry chest hair that she wanted to run her fingers through. Then there was the way his black trousers hugged his butt and his thighs.

God, the man was sexy enough to make a corpse feel things. And she was very much alive, her body coming back to itself with delicious little pangs.

He shaved in quick, deft movements, washed, pulled on another crisp white shirt. As if remembering her presence, he turned and frowned. "Get into the water. It will get cold."

"I will, after you leave," she said, pulling the lapels of her damp robe together. The motion only caused his gaze to slip down, noting how the silk hugged her breasts.

His eyes darkened, and satisfaction that she pleased him made her flush. God, was there anything this man didn't make her feel?

"I watched you give birth to our son. There's nothing to…" He stopped himself and shook his head. "Forgive me. Two more minutes and I'll be out of your hair."

She nodded, soft heat streaking her cheeks.

Intimacy swirled around them like an invisible dome, trapping them inside. Plus, it was intensely pleasurable to watch Renzo dress. He did it with a meticulous efficiency, like he did everything else. Still, the thought that *only she* was getting a behind-the-scenes show filled her with perverse, unjustified satisfaction.

Until another thought struck. "You're going out," she said, following him into the bedroom, her voice sharp enough to make him pause.

A black jacket lay on the chaise behind him, and the

gleam of polished leather shoes by his feet told her everything she needed to know.

He looked up, his fingers busy fastening the cuff links on his shirt. "It's a business dinner. Something I can't skip tonight."

Mimi stared at him and nodded slowly. Her throat tightened, and she let out a shaky breath. "Those Japanese investors that your assistant was talking about."

Surprise painted his features. He finished his cuff link with a decisive snap and stepped toward her. "I'll only be gone for a few hours. Unless you need me here. Or there's something I haven't thought of."

His gray eyes held hers for several beats, willing her to say something. Anything.

"No," Mimi said, sounding more decisive than she felt. "You've arranged everything I could possibly need. There's nothing more."

His Adam's apple moved. "I'll see you in the morning then," he said, picking up his jacket.

The door closed behind him with a soft click, and Mimi stared for long minutes at the space he had just occupied. The room felt cavernous without him, the quiet pressing down on her like a weight.

Would it be just the investors he was seeing? Or would he seek other forms of entertainment? And if he did let loose after the last stressful month, did she have any right to question in what form he sought that relief and release?

She had admitted the inevitable conclusion of their attraction, but that didn't mean a virile, attractive man like Renzo would wait for her, did it? Nor would a sophisticated man like him limit himself to her. It wasn't as if their vows actually meant anything. Not unless she asked him for exclusivity and fidelity in their marriage.

She clenched her hands in the folds of her robe, her heart warring with itself. How much of her whirling thoughts was the truth and how much was her self-preservation kicking in?

He had clearly admitted to wanting her, to wanting to make this marriage real. Would he be so cheap as to pursue another woman while she was recovering from childbirth?

At least she could have asked him to stay and keep her company on this first night away from their son. He had wanted her to ask him. She was sure of that too.

But her stubbornness, and the knee-jerk instinct to protect herself, had stopped her.

This marriage wasn't about love or comfort or their individual needs.

It was a convenience, a practical solution to their complex situation. Already, the pregnancy and the delivery had made a maudlin fool out of her. But enough was enough.

Luca was getting stronger every day and would soon come home. It was better all around if she started planning her life separately from her husband's. For that's what they would lead.

And yet as she shed her robe and sank into the deliciously hot water, her heart ached desperately for him to hold her just one more time. To give herself into his capable arms completely. Her entire being yearned to make this marriage, their relationship, real on every level possible.

CHAPTER SEVEN

Renzo returned to a dark, silent penthouse barely an hour later.

He did have out-of-town investors to wine and dine, people he had fobbed on his two assistants in the past week because he hadn't wanted to leave Luca or Mimi at the hospital.

Even if he had stolen away for an evening, he wouldn't have been good company.

Tonight's dinner was important.

And yet he had known he'd made the wrong choice the moment he'd stepped foot into their Hotel DiCarlo Palazzo, overlooking the Grand Canal.

His wife needed him but was too stubborn to admit it or ask him for anything. And he...was just as stubborn, wanting her to come to him, wanting her to seek something, anything, from him. *Cristo*, the woman could twist him up, inside out, without even trying.

Events of the last few months had been the most intense and draining experiences of his life. He couldn't begin to imagine how much more it must have cost her. Losing her sister, deciding to keep the baby, taking care of herself and then standing up to him even as she married him.

There was no doubt that his wife was an exceptional woman. And strong-willed to the core.

But she was also young and fragile, despite her every effort to act the opposite of the latter.

He glared at the large empty bed in the master bedroom, then proceeded to the two guest bedrooms. Only darkness greeted him in both. Frowning, he pushed the heavy doors of his study open.

His chest gave a painful twinge as his eyes found her small form tucked deep into his heavy armchair, fast asleep. He switched on the desk lamp, his breath coming in rough exhales as he recognized the gray sweatshirt she'd draped over herself.

It was his.

With her hair in a braid and wisps framing her face, she looked small and innocent.

The sight of her sleeping form, her nose and chin tucked against the fabric, did things to him he didn't understand. He roughly thrust a hand through his hair, a wave of tenderness shaking him from the inside.

Feeling things for her wasn't in his equation for this marriage. And yet he didn't know how to stop.

Bending, he gently scooped her into his arms and lifted her.

Instantly, she nuzzled her face into his neck as if they had taken part in this very same ritual a thousand nights before. Her trust in him, in such a vulnerable state, when she was such a prickly little thing usually, pacified some age-old instinct in him that only she called forth.

The lush rose scent, deepened by her skin, filled his lungs by the time he brought her to the bed in his bedroom. He had barely tucked her under the duvet, one knee by her side, when those beautiful brown eyes flickered open. In the moonlight filtering through the French windows, her lashes cast shadows against her cheeks, her skin smooth and gleaming.

Her fingers fisted his shirt, lush lips puffing out air. Slowly, she became aware of her surroundings. "Renzo?"

"Sleep, Mimi," he said, pressing a quick kiss to her forehead. *Dio mio*, he couldn't control the simplest urge around this woman. "The armchair in my study is hardly convenient for a night's sleep."

A soft, maybe even dreamy, smile curved her lips. "You can't help chastising me, can you?"

"You can't help fighting me, can you?"

"Not fighting in this case, Renzo," she said, her smile touching her eyes now. "It's the only room in the penthouse that smells like you. Citrus and bergamot." She blinked as if realizing what she had said. Then sighed.

Her warm, minty breath coated his chin. And if he could just nudge her chin up, he could taste her again. The last time they had kissed had been when Luca had been born, and her kiss had tasted of salt and tears and sweat.

Renzo had loved it.

But he wanted to kiss her again, when she was soft and dreamy like this. When she was fuming and mouthy with him. When she fought him at every inch.

He wanted to know how his wife tasted in every mood, like the shades of a rainbow. *Dio mio*, he was a gone case.

"I...didn't want to be alone," she whispered, and yet there was a new clarity to her tone that he hadn't seen since that day he had found her.

He tugged his gaze upward. "Understandable, *bella*."

"All the beds, including this one, were cold and sterile. One of the guest bedrooms smelled like perfume." She scrunched her brow. "Is this where you bring your lovers, Renzo?" She stiffened, looking around her, as if she could find a lover of his lurking under the bed. Ire flashed in her eyes, but when she spoke, her voice was steady. "I understand you have a life, but bringing me to your stud pad is hardly appropriate."

He smiled. "My bed is cold and sterile probably because I haven't slept here in a month. A laundering service comes in and changes everything once a week. And no, I've never brought a lover here. This is my sanctuary." He waited for his answer to sink in. "As for the guest bedroom, my sister was here a few days ago. It's possible she slept in there."

"Chiara was here? In Venice?" She tried to hide it, but an instant wariness clouded her eyes. "I thought she and her husband lived in Milan."

"She came up to see Luca and you. Without informing me of her decision."

His wife's swallow was audible.

Renzo cursed himself and his whole family inwardly. Every single one of them, including his usually kind mother, had taken their cue from his distaste and dislike of Pia and her entire family.

Only now it dawned on him that both Santo and Pia were responsible for their volatile marriage, not just the latter.

He wouldn't be surprised if Chiara had snubbed Mimi a hundred times during holiday and family gatherings in the last six years. And his own arrogant judgment was responsible for it.

"I didn't see her at the hospital," Mimi said in a small voice.

"She never came to the hospital. I sent her away."

"Oh. Why?"

"Neither you nor Luca is ready for anyone's visits or scrutiny, *bella*. Not even my family. I told your mother the same."

She threw herself at him like a child, her arms going around his waist. The scent of her hair, the press of her body turned him rock-hard. *Merda*, but he was a selfish, needy bastard.

She had given birth a month ago, and here he was, lusting after her body. The thought was so jarring that he frowned.

His lust for her was more than just for her body. It was for her mind, her soul even. He wanted to own this woman like he'd never owned anything else. He wanted her to belong to him without doubt, and he wanted her to want to belong to him.

He wanted her every waking thought to be consumed by him. He wanted her loyalty, her strength, her desires to belong to him.

"Thank you. That might be the best present you've ever given me."

"I haven't given you anything," he said, clamping his fingers gently around her nape. Her curves were soft and warm against him, notching the tension in his muscles tighter. "Not even a wedding present." He'd heard one of the nurses tease her about what gifts he had given her on the occasion of their son's birth and seen the sudden dismay before she made up a lie about a necklace.

A wedding present hadn't been necessary, he reminded

himself. Nor had he had the time for it. And knowing her, she would have hated the pretense of one. And yet… some foolish, apparently sentimental part of him wished he had given her something. Anything. A small token that was meant just for her and not the fact that she was carrying his child.

She shrugged, cheek resting against his chest. "Don't need anything more than this right now. More than the three of us."

He stroked her back lightly, swallowing at the heat of her body sending tingles up his hand. He cleared his throat, hoping to dislodge the need coiling inside him. At some point, real life would intrude on their bubble, and he had to prepare her for it.

"At some point, we'll have to do a press release about him. Maybe a photo shoot. And my family will insist on visiting. My mother especially…" He swallowed the sudden lump in his throat. Still, his words came out scratchy. "She is eager to see her grandson. Please…" he nearly choked on the word, but he couldn't forget that he had a duty to others too "…consider the fact that she's just lost her firstborn."

Of late though, he was beginning to resent the emotional cost of managing his mother's grief, his sister's disappointment in her marriage, and his father's spurious guilt, which would undoubtedly launch him into impulsive behavior and another scandal.

This cocoon he had been in for the last few weeks, with only Luca and Mimi and some work as his focus, had been a luxury he hadn't known he needed.

Her breath warm against his neck, Mimi looked up. The smile was gone from her face, replaced by that shadow of a grief he knew too well. "Of course. I...like your mother. Maybe in another week? Hopefully I'll be less of a wreck then."

"You like my mother?" Renzo blurted out before he could stop himself. "In a week is more than I hoped for." He ran his knuckles down her soft cheek. "I was ready to give you another month."

"She was always kind to me. And with Pia, she never added fuel to the arguments or the drama. I understood her perspective that she wanted Santo to be happy and thought he was being trod over."

"How are you so wise at such a young age?"

She laughed, and Renzo thought it was the most beautiful sight he had ever seen. "Practice, my pupil." And then she giggled at her own joke. "You're forgetting that I'm also very strategic. Your mother had four children. She might be a fount of important advice about babies. And I want Luca to know his family, to be surrounded by so much love that he never doubts it."

"And you wonder why I insisted on marrying you?" he quipped. The sheer longing in her voice as she talked about Luca knowing love was...unmistakable. "You're already a fierce mother to him."

This time, the smile he wanted didn't bloom. Nodding, she pulled back, her gaze skating everywhere but at him. And Renzo wondered where he had made a misstep in the last minute. "As for you being a wreck, it won't get better unless you rest properly."

"Wait, I forgot to ask." She released his shirt and looked up. "What happened at your meeting? Why are you back so soon?"

"It got rescheduled," he lied automatically.

"Lucky for me." Her teasing only tightened the tension in his body. When he tried to pull his arm away, her clasp firmed.

"I need a shower, *bella*."

Pulling herself up with her grip on his arm—which of course made her grimace—she leaned close, tucked her face in his chest and took a deep breath. "You smell fine to me. More than fine, in fact. You smell great. Always do."

He shook his head, a short huff of exasperation escaping him. "Mimi..."

"Stay with me, Renzo." Then, pushing the wild strands of hair out of her face, she patted the space beside her on the bed. "I was being stubborn and foolish earlier. I don't want to be alone in this cavernous apartment. No, that's not specific enough." Her brown eyes shimmered with resolve. "I want to go to sleep with your arms around me."

When he simply stared at her, her shoulders rounded in defeat. "You want me to beg? Is that it?"

"Of course not," he said, moving up on the bed. If he lay down on the bed with her, he wasn't sure he could hide his need from her. His body would betray him with one press of her slender curves against him. And he loathed the idea of coming on to her when she was in such a fragile state, when she was asking him for companionship and comfort.

He loathed how out of control he was near her. And this would not do. Not if he wanted a successful, amiable marriage. He couldn't be at the mercy of his desires. Not now, not ever.

When she was ready for their relationship to move on

to the next step, that was different. But as her husband, he could not deny her what she sought from him now.

"I have a few hours of work to get through." He pressed a finger to her lips when she'd have protested. "But I'll stay here until you fall asleep. Then shower and work, *sì*?"

"*Grazie*, Renzo," she whispered.

Averting his gaze from hers, he scooted up the bed and pulled her into his side. Her palm came to rest on his abdomen, and it took everything he had to not fidget, to not scoop her completely into his arms. To not slide into the bed fully and spoon her from head to toe until she was engulfed in him.

Dio mio, he wasn't even fond of cuddling, had never even tried it. But already, he liked holding her this way, even without satisfaction for his body's torment.

He set his other hand to stroke her forehead. Soon her breathing deepened.

Tilting his head back against the headboard, he closed his eyes, running through all the work and family stuff piling up for him.

All the bullet points on his list evaded him, though. For he had never known the sweet contentment that filled him with Mimi's hands tightly wrapped around his.

It shouldn't have been so easy to settle into a rhythm over the next month, but they did. In just three days, Luca would be two months old. And each day, he was getting stronger and that much closer to coming home to them.

Four weeks since Mimi had moved to the penthouse, and it might as well have been four decades for how easily she and Renzo seemed to slot into each other's lives with minimal adjustments.

Or maybe she shouldn't be surprised, Mimi thought, given Renzo turned out to be the most accommodating man on the planet.

Contrary to all that she'd feared about sharing a space with him and his overbearing personality, the man went out of his way to make sure her every need was attended to, before even she realized she had it.

For someone who had looked after herself most of her life, it was…disconcerting to be such a focal point of someone else's attention. Not that she was very different from an important project, and Renzo was managing her with his usual ruthless expertise.

It bothered her more with each passing day. She didn't know what she wanted—and how she hated not knowing herself—but the very polite, very rational shape their relationship had taken grated on her, day and night. As did the increasingly static nature of her day.

Each morning, a hot breakfast—optimized for her maximum well-being—would be waiting for her the exact moment she came into the kitchen, after a shower and a round of stretches with her coach.

The latter was honestly a luxury she wished she could afford the rest of her life. She didn't care so much about losing her mommy pooch, as she'd taken to calling it, but she loved how light and less sore her body felt after the stretches.

Dressed in a designer suit, jet-black hair slicked back, Renzo would be chugging some disgusting protein shake. He never left for work without greeting her in the morning. Usually, she pushed her breakfast around the plate, trying to think of something witty or funny to say.

Then they went to the clinic together, where he asked

the specialist for updates on Luca and then translated every word to her with the patience of a saint. He then kissed her on the cheek before leaving for work, the exact same place every day.

As if X marked the spot. As if the world might cave in if he deviated or lingered a second too long.

Then somewhere around noon, she drifted to the guest suite reserved specifically for her at the clinic, ate lunch half-heartedly, napped as if she'd run a full marathon, then went to see Luca and hold him for a little while.

Just as the sun began to set, the chauffeur brought her home. She showered, stretched, ate dinner, caught up on her favorite murder mysteries on TV and then went to bed. And somehow, every night, Renzo showed up right as she struggled to fall asleep.

He uncuffed his shirt sleeves, undid his tie, and crawled into bed with her, but never held her fully. As if someone had stuck a huge rod in his back that stopped him from bending it.

Some nights, he looked haggard and disheveled, like last night. Other nights, he would be brimming with energy, having secured some deal or achieved a milestone, and Mimi would fall asleep to the gravelly tone of his voice.

As if he had crafted her very own lullaby with that deep, chocolate-melting voice.

That he kept his promise to her soothed some neglected part of her soul, but it was limited to his one hand in her hair and his hard, corded form next to her if she needed it.

Just last night, she had nuzzled her face into the outside of his thigh, after a particularly nasty nightmare about Luca. Of course, he had pulled her up into his arms, whispered words she didn't understand in that musical lilt, pressed soft kisses to her forehead until she calmed down and drifted back to sleep.

It was as if he had turned into her personal sleeping drug, and she was already addicted to him. Mimi's cheeks heated. The hard clench of his sleek thigh muscle as she nearly tried to climb him was imprinted on her forever.

These were her thoughts as she stepped into the spacious breakfast nook another same, slow morning.

The nook was her favorite space in the massive penthouse. From her perch on the leather seat, she could see the canals' shimmering waters reflecting the pastel facades of historic buildings. Gondolas glided by, their rhythmic strokes a quiet counterpoint to the distant toll of church bells and beyond, the horizon opened to the sparkling expanse of the Adriatic Sea.

The history lover in her was dying to explore all the corners of the city. It struck her, as if she were walking out of a mist, that she was free to explore. While it soothed some elemental part of her to be at the clinic all hours, to be close to Luca in case he needed her, she was also slowly going mad. It was the reason her sleep was so fitful, for she simply drifted from one day to the next.

She'd always worked, even when she'd been finishing her bachelor's in filmmaking. Wary of spending a minute more than necessary at her parents' house, caught amid Pia's or her mom's drama, she had filled her days with work, studies and friends. If nothing else, she'd pack up her camera equipment any given weekend and wander around new cities and towns, shooting everyday places and people. She had to do that now.

If she hoped to remain sane over the next few weeks,

it was important to retain and nurture those parts of herself. God, she adored her son with a breathless wonder that would never dim, but she needed to look after her own well-being too. Much as it was nice to be coddled by Renzo, that wasn't his job.

"I want to explore the city. Can you find me a map?" she blurted out, refusing to overthink it. She had to start something today, to break the rigid monotony stretching endlessly ahead of her.

Across the marble-topped table with its vase of rust-colored chrysanthemums and golden sunflowers, Renzo, in his stark black suit, looked stark and uncompromising. And all the more beautiful for it. And her libido, a sneaky, snaky thing, uncoiled and took notice.

He straightened in the leather seat, a line forming between his brows.

It was one of those little details about him that seemed to elevate the man from merely good-looking to something otherworldly. Like that misplaced little dimple near his upper lip and the little scar that bifurcated his left eyebrow just so.

A host of imperfections crafting him into a perfectly stunning man.

One of those devilish brows hitched up at her leisurely perusal of his face. Cheeks burning, Mimi took a hasty sip of her coffee and nearly hissed when the hot brew hit her throat.

"Is there something particular you want to see?" he said after long, suffocating minutes of staring at her.

"Do you have only one boat?" she snapped, reacting to that high-handedness like a child.

His frown deepened. "No. I own six boats, *cara*, and

they are all at your disposal. Transportation, as you should know, is not the problem."

"Then what is?"

"I can't have you roaming the city by yourself. For one thing, you're new to it. For another, you will be recognized and mobbed, and you are…"

"I'm what? A foolish, bug-eyed tourist who can't look after myself?" It was her turn to raise her brow, and she did it magnificently. "Also, I really don't have that memorable a face."

"You're my wife and a DiCarlo. There will always be someone who's interested in you." He put his fork down with exaggerated patience and then set that gaze on her. Mimi felt like a target in some survivor game. It was crazy how dizzy his gaze made her. "You're picking a fight with me. Why?"

That perceptive statement took the wind out of her sails. And she knew, in her sloshing belly, that he was right. That she wanted more from him and didn't want to. Didn't even know how or what to ask for. "I just want to do something for myself," she said, neither confirming nor denying his claim.

"Something for yourself…" he repeated, as if tasting and testing the words on his lips.

"Is it such an alien concept?" she said softly, irritation building in her chest. "I'm going stir-crazy waiting for Luca to come home. I need to do something to break the monotony, to get back to my work. And Venice is such an interesting city. Just for collecting some footage. And all I'm asking you for is some guidance as to where to start."

"You don't want to take it easy for a little longer?"

"Can you imagine sitting around at home for days on

end without nothing to do? Caught in this strange limbo where life isn't moving forward?"

The concept must have sounded so bizarre to him that he nodded. "I see what you mean."

"I'm not used to doing nothing. Wandering the city's just an idea."

"If you can wait until the weekend, I will show you around."

Her hackles rose immediately. "You don't have to babysit me. Nor do I want to force my company on you."

A sudden flash of anger danced in his eyes, but of course, he didn't let it rise. And she wondered, for the hundredth time in the last couple of months, what would happen if Renzo lost control. If he let his emotions, and desires, rule him instead of his head. "In case you've forgotten, we are married, *cara*. Spending time with you is hardly an imposition. If anything, it's one of the requirements of this marriage, *si*?"

And there it was, that word, *imposition*.

She *was* an imposition on him, his lifestyle, his space, no matter how much he denied it. It was only duty and honor that dictated his behavior.

She had been an imposition on her mother who had only wanted to purse her acting career without a child holding her back. An imposition on her MIA sperm-donor father who hadn't wanted anything to do with an unexpected baby.

She had been an imposition on Pia when all she had wanted was for father to remain hers.

God, just when she thought her hormones had flatlined and she could return to normal, these...twisted feelings snuck up on her.

But she knew, as surely as the longing in her body, that things were changing each day, and she was running to catch up to her own feelings. "I appreciate your offer. But I would like to do it alone," she said, keeping her tone steady.

His jaw ticked as seconds slowly rippled by.

"You do realize I don't need your permission, right?"

"You're forever trying to push the boundaries between us, *si*?" he said silkily.

"I'm trying to stay behind those boundaries, Renzo. You're the one who…"

He leaned forward, the predator ready to pounce. "I'm the one what, *bella*?"

Mimi shook her head. She was being unfair to him. Just because it was possible that he had lost all the interest in her that he had claimed before their wedding. Maybe seeing her give birth had put him off, she thought with a hysterical edge.

Falling back into her seat, she closed her eyes, arresting the ridiculous tears that came knocking.

Firm fingers on her shoulders made her straighten and then moan as they kneaded her muscles with the perfect pressure. That delicious, decadent scent of him coated her throat, making her body tingle. She was so helpless against his simplest touch.

"How about we make a deal?" he said. Something droll danced in his tone. "It seems the best way for us to navigate this…partnership."

Her eyes flicked open. The dimple by his upper lip beckoned her touch, the perfect bow shape of his lips alluringly close.

He was upside down to her gaze and just as gloriously

gorgeous. There was a part of her that wanted to commit this spiraling attraction, this simmering desire for him, as her own body and mind trying to find the normal again after the life-changing event of her son's birth.

But Renzo DiCarlo, she had to admit, would always render her knees weak, make her body hot and drown her heart in foolish longings. The first two she was fine with. It was the last that gave her pause.

His eyes seemed infinitely deep as he said, "That way, you can feel like you're in control of this."

"What kind of deal?" she said, feeling as if she were splayed out for his amusement.

His fingers moved up to clasp her cheeks. "You join me for an intimate dinner with two of my closest friends, and I will let your bodyguard, Enrico, take you to an antique notebook shop that's been standing for nearly a hundred years. You're interested in history and culture and art, right?"

"You're a tease," she said, her breath a wispy thing.

He laughed, and the lines fanning out across his sharp features looked like a map to a treasure. Her very own private treasure, if only she could reach her hand out towards it. "You're easy to tease, *cara*."

"Just two friends?"

"Sì."

"Okay. This antique notebook shop, can you arrange an interview for me with the owner? Perhaps I could document the history of the shop."

His eyes gleamed as if he had known she would ask exactly that. "Will you promise to stick to that one place for today?"

"Fine."

"Good girl," he said with a tap to her cheek, then released her.

Dampness bloomed between her thighs, and Mimi gasped at the sheer pleasure of the sensation curling deep within her. It had been a while—a long while—since her body had reacted with such a jolt of need that she felt dizzy.

Renzo's hand waiting to pull her up was less an anchor and more another stimulus.

Straightening, she watched him as he finished his coffee, collected his suit jacket, pressed another kiss to that spot on her cheek and hurried out.

She didn't want to read much into the fact that he had known how much she would like to visit the antique notebook shop. But she had a feeling he'd been holding that card for a while.

With the intention of...persuading her to meet his friends? Or to simply give her the pleasure of the visit? Could her ruthless, powerful, busy billionaire of a husband have given thought to what would make her happy?

And more importantly, why did her heart flutter like a caged bird at the thought of Renzo caring about her?

CHAPTER EIGHT

THE EVENING OF their dinner with Renzo's friends snuck up on Mimi, leaving her staring blankly at the meager selection in her wardrobe.

She was never going to be as good as the elite set that Renzo called friends, but she didn't want to embarrass herself or him by proxy.

Of course, she should have known that her very efficient husband would not only foresee her little problem but arrange a prompt solution. Multiple outfits, along with sophisticated accessories and shoes, had been delivered right to their penthouse an hour before he'd informed her he would pick her up later that night.

Suddenly, she understood what an embarrassment of riches meant.

Silk A-line dresses with cashmere shawls in warm earth colors greeted her eyes. Her heart beat out a staccato rhythm as she realized he'd noted she didn't wear too-bright, dazzling clothes.

His powers of observation and his perception, his ability to see her as she was…astounded and aroused her equally.

Bright colors and daring outfits had been Pia's domain. Since there had never been a chance that she could outshine her stepsister—nor did she want to declare a challenge that she was trying to—Mimi had always picked earthy, jewel tones. Also, as a documentary maker, it helped to blend into the surroundings, to put her subjects at ease and to gain their confidence on hard subjects.

And now, staring at herself in the full-length mirror, Mimi amended the narrative in her head.

From the moment she'd understood Pia's nature, those muted colors had felt safe. But now, it was what she preferred, she told herself.

She would always be the woman behind the camera, watching life wield its magic in the most mundane moments and recording it for posterity. It didn't, however, mean that she played it safe or that she was afraid of standing out.

Grief struck her like sudden lightning flashing across the sky. Would Pia have been more reasonable if Mimi had learned to assert herself early on in their relationship? If she had refused to give in to her every whim so easily? If she'd just believed in herself a little more and been stronger? If her mom had taken her side and disciplined Pia's extreme demands and tantrums?

Would Pia have been alive today?

Groaning, Mimi fell onto the bed, next to the neat piles of her new wardrobe.

Would these thoughts ever stop haunting her? Could she and Renzo ever make this work for each other with such guilt and grief hanging over them? Was that what she wanted for the future—Renzo as her partner, her lover, her husband for real?

Suddenly, she felt far too fragile to expose herself to Renzo's friends and their scrutiny. In addition to his.

Then her gaze fell on the last outfit.

It was a single-breasted tuxedo-inspired pantsuit in a emerald green, crafted from a luxe crepe material. The jacket had a plunging neckline with satin lapels and a cinched waist. It looked like it had been made for her, in body type and color and fabric.

High-waisted slim trousers with a subtle flare to them immediately accentuated her long legs as she pulled them up over silk panties.

She tied the dramatic black silk sash belt at her waist and sighed. The belt added a hint of femininity to her structured look, which was her exact preferred style. Her usual bold red lipstick added a splash of color, and she finished with a slightly smoky eye. Her long hair—her crowning glory—she left in its naturally glossy waves down her back.

Put together, she looked effortlessly glamorous, two words she would have never applied to herself. And all thanks to Renzo's thoughtfulness. *He can't have you embarrassing him*, whispered that sneaky, distrustful voice that had always urged her to back down with Pia.

With a shake of her head, Mimi shut it down. The last thing she'd ever wanted in life was to become this...negative person who never trusted good things happening to her. But clearly she had. And that wouldn't do, not for her, and not for Luca.

Renzo had been more thoughtful and attentive than she'd ever imagined, and she wasn't going to ruin it with old patterns of thinking.

It was time to move forward, away from the grief and guilt, time to embrace her own desires and wants.

* * *

The private launch glided smoothly through the Venetian lagoon, its polished mahogany hull gleaming under the moonlight.

Mimi sat on one of the cream leather seats, the buttery-soft material cool beneath her fingers. The interior was a masterclass in luxury, with brass accents on the handrails and a small built-in bar stocked with sparkling water and champagne.

Outside, the rhythmic hum of the engine was a soft counterpoint to the gentle lapping of water against the hull.

Lanterns strung along nearby buildings cast shimmering reflections on the water, creating a kaleidoscope of colors that danced around them as they passed.

But the magnificent beauty all around her paled in front of the man sitting across from her.

She should be used to Renzo's sensual appeal, and yet her belly sloshed with fizzy tingles near him. Even if she could fight the attraction on a physical level, the fact that she was beginning to like him and admire him was another thing altogether.

Overdelivering on his promise, he had had her bodyguard, Enrico, escort her to the most interesting places in the city all week—off-the-wall places imbued with history and art. She couldn't deny the gut feeling that he had chosen those places specifically with her in mind. That he knew her.

It was exactly what she'd needed to find her footing again, to spark her own creativity back to life. She'd shot so much B-roll and had been editing and playing with it when he returned to the penthouse at night. There had been no cuddling in the bed, and she had lost even that little contact with him.

For the last two nights, though, he hadn't returned home at all, and she had eventually slipped into a restless slumber.

Now, with his long legs stretched out casually, his focus was anything but relaxed. From the moment he had seen her step out of the penthouse elevator, something had come over him. He hadn't even paid her a compliment, and it pinched.

Pity she had never learned the art of decoding powerful, breathtakingly handsome men like Pia had.

But she wanted to understand this one desperately.

His dark eyes rested on her even now, intense and searching, making her feel more exposed than the low neckline of her jacket ever could.

"Is everything okay at work?" she said, her voice thankfully breezy. She'd had a lot of practice with burying her emotions under a calm facade, and yet she was sure it was becoming a barrier with Renzo that she didn't want to keep up. "You didn't come home for two nights."

"Are you thinking of the penthouse as home now, *bella*?"

"That's not an answer to my question."

Renzo's eyes narrowed slightly, but instead of replying, he looked out toward the horizon. The rhythmic hum of the engine filled the silence, accompanied by the faint scents of brine and of roses from the gardens lining the canal.

Mimi let the moment stretch, wary of pressing further but wanting to know.

He rubbed a long finger over his temple, his hesitation

crystal clear. "Massimo got into trouble with some rival fraternity club at uni and ended up in jail."

Her mouth fell open, and she snapped it shut. "Is he okay? Did you get him out?"

"Not the first night, no."

"Oh." She frowned, confused. "Pia used to go on about how powerful your family was. Which I now realize is mostly you. But you weren't able to get him released?"

A half smile touched his lips but didn't reach his eyes. At least the reason behind his brooding was partly clear. "Pia was right. I slogged to build up the DiCarlo name to what it used to be during my grandfather's reign. But Massimo, like my father, has gotten used to that privilege far too much. From everything I learned, he was the one who started that fight after several warnings from the provost. Beating someone up as if he were a street thug…" A vein pulsed in his temple. Exhaustion coated his words when he spoke again. "He deserved to rot in jail for both nights and learn a lesson, but Mama's tears were endless. I got him out after thirty-six hours."

Mimi's stood up suddenly, eager to touch him. She nearly toppled into him before he steadied her with his hands on her hips. "I'm sorry that you had to make such a hard decision," she said, sitting by him. "But I'm sure it's for his own good."

"Such implicit trust, Mimi?" His lips quirked into a tight smile. "Even my own family won't afford me that. Papa…" the one word dropped into the silence with all the weight of a thousand-pound anchor "…whipped them all into a frenzy about how harsh and ruthless I was growing. Apparently, all this power is going to my head. And

Massimo should be forgiven however many mistakes he makes because he's of the tender age of twenty-two."

Her heart ached for the sliver of hurt in those words. "I don't care what they think. But I do trust you, Renzo. Luca's fortunate to have a father like you. Santo would have loved him, but you will also teach him how to be a good man."

He looked so stunned that she felt heat creeping into her cheeks. "If I haven't made that abundantly clear already, I'm sorry." She tapped his knuckles gently. "Our son is very lucky. As am I, at least temporarily." She hated adding the last bit but forced herself to. It tasted like dust on her tongue.

He gave a curt nod and again, that tension rolled back in like a relentless cresting wave.

"Will you be gone for more nights?" she asked, trying and failing to not sound like a clingy wife.

"Probably not." He pushed his hand through his hair, though the movement lacked the usual grace. "But there's mountains of work to get through, and you seem to—"

"Why do you never lie down fully beside me? Why do you always leave, whatever the time of the night?" She was needling him. And he didn't deserve it, tonight of all nights. But she couldn't stop.

Perhaps it was the way the moonlight caught the hard lines of his jaw, or the fact that their little cocoon was gone, and she was stepping into his world. She wanted some token of connection between them before they were swallowed up by the world and even Luca.

The realization both startled and freed her.

He stared at her, as shocked at her questions as she herself was. His mouth worked, as did his Adam's apple, framed by the white collar of his shirt. Mimi had the most maddening urge to press her mouth there.

"Are you allergic to sleeping by someone?" she taunted him to cover up her own nerves. "Does no woman on the planet get the full Renzo DiCarlo treatment?"

Another half smile and then a roll of those hard shoulders. "You want the truth?"

"Yes, please." She laced her fingers in her lap. "Whatever it is, I can take it."

"I didn't want to make you aware of my...ever-present desire." Self-deprecation coated each word. "I'm furious with Massimo for having no control over his temper, and yet my body behaves like a teenager around you. After everything you've been through these past few months, it feels crass to even hint at what I would like to do to you. Even subconsciously."

It was the last thing she had expected, and she felt like a floundering fish out of her depth. But they had come this far, and she wasn't going back. "What do you want to do to me, Renzo?"

His gray eyes flashed with such simmering heat that her belly flip-flopped again. "So that you can call yourself the victor in this battle?"

"What? No. Of course not." She was so eager to make him understand that she nearly crawled into his lap. "Renzo... I've been worried that I was clinging to you and stifling you with my demands and forcing my hands onto your rock-hard abdomen every night. I even wondered if whatever attraction we had before wore off on your side because you saw me give me birth, and then I had to take off points from you for being that shallow.

God, all these days…all I wanted was to beg you for just one more kiss, and—"

She got her wish without having to beg.

His soft, cold lips trapped hers in a hard, hot kiss that made a hundred champagne bottles fizz open in her belly. Large hands cupped her hips and easily lifted her until she was sitting sideways in his lap. The shocking evidence of his half-mast erection made her gasp, and he swooped in, tasting, licking every corner of her mouth. As if he meant to plant his flag there and declare it his kingdom.

He cornered the tip of her tongue and sucked at it with such expertise that her toes curled in her pumps. The twin feelings of being tethered to the ground while flying overcame her. She clamped her arm around his shoulders, trying to burrow into him.

"Come, Mimi. Play with me," he said in that commanding voice that could melt her insides like they were made of chocolate, and she lost the last layer of inhibition.

Sinking her fingers into his hair, Mimi kissed him with all the pent-up desire she had been feeling for months now. Each rub and slide of their lips sent a spark shooting through her, teaching her about her own body's new contours and fresh needs. The taste of him—whiskey and sin—filled her to overflowing. She felt like a new woman in a new body, even one with a little wear and tear.

For the first time in her life, she was doing what she wanted, without a thought to anyone else's wishes.

Just her needs. Only her desires.

Wanton heat bloomed when she shifted in his lap and his thick, hot erection rolled against her hip. The sound that burst out of his throat was like a feral animal's, and it sent savage shivers through her. That she could arouse this powerful, gorgeous man to such heights of desire… made power thrum through her. Her arousal deepened into something more, stoked by the affection and admiration she felt for him. He was the first person in the world who had paid real attention to her, who cared what she wanted and saw her like no one ever had.

Every guttural sound he made, every harsh breath that escaped those sinuous lips, she bottled it all up like a female dragon hoarding her treasure.

"And here I thought you were an innocent minx I would corrupt with my desires," he murmured at her ear before licking the shell.

Shivering, she rolled her hips against that thickness again. In return, that dampness bloomed between her thighs. It drenched her flimsy lace panties, and that in itself was another new, decadent sensation. "It's your own fault for making assumptions." An ache pulsed at her core, fanned into a bigger flame with his roving, stroking hands and teasing lips, begging to be put out.

God, she couldn't remember the last time she had been this turned on by a simple kiss. Although there was nothing simple about how Renzo devoured her. Like everything else about him, his desire was overpowering, addictive.

Biting out a curse, he pulled back and pressed his forehead to hers. "Contrary to our pre-wedding kiss, I don't want the bloody world and the media to witness this one, *bella*."

"Hmm…" Mimi said, still riding the delirious high of his kiss.

When he grinned—which rendered him even more gorgeous—she looked around. The launch was approaching the private dock of the Grand DiCarlo Venezia. It rose like a palace from the water, its grand facade illuminated by soft golden lights.

But even the sight of the imposing hotel couldn't dim her awareness of the man holding her like she was fragile while his kisses were filthy.

"And here I thought you were all about the performance, Mr. DiCarlo."

Groaning, he gently pushed her to her feet while surreptitiously arranging his trousers. "I think you should hold off on giving me a rating, Mrs. DiCarlo."

She giggled, and his gaze swept over her face. A small but utterly genuine smile played about his own lips.

On impulse, Mimi threw herself at him and kissed that smile, desperate for a taste of it. "Your smile...it does things to me," she whispered, then hid her face in his neck. "Even worse than your voice." His laughter was a rumble against her body, both comforting and arousing. "I think I know what I want for a wedding present."

His fingers gently nudged her back. "What?"

"More of what we just did. I...like how I feel when you kiss me."

His thumb traced her cheekbone. "How much more?"

"A lot more. All of it if we can manage it." Then, because she couldn't be anything but honest, she said, "I'm nervous, but I also want this. For you and me."

"Ahhh...*cara*. Fate picked you to torment me, *sì*?" In one second, the passionate lover transformed into the caring partner who had held her hand through hours of labor. His mouth was at her temple again. "I don't want to rush you into anything yet, *bella*. We have a lifetime for all the filthy, wicked things I want to do to you."

"Do we?" The words tumbled out of her before she could stop them, propelled by an urgent desperation to know if things had changed for him. "Our agreement was for one year."

A harsh laugh escaped him. "It's never anything less than a battle with you, is it?"

"Renzo, wait—"

"Let's not argue in front of the whole world. I refuse to follow in Santo and Pia's footsteps. Everything that happens between us remains between us, *si*?"

It was a sentiment Mimi could get behind, so she swallowed her protest and nodded.

The hotel was a masterpiece. The hum of the boat faded as the launch docked at the private pier, and Mimi's heart fluttered with nerves.

She'd known Renzo's company owned luxury resorts, but seeing one up close like this was overwhelming. "This is one of yours?" she asked, her voice low.

"Ours, *bella*," he said, standing as the boat came to a stop. "The jewel in the crown of the DiCarlo empire."

He extended a hand to her, and for a moment she hesitated before taking it. His touch was warm, grounding, and despite his tight jaw, she felt a flicker of gratitude for his steady presence through everything. "Before you argue with me, the penthouse is home now, *si*? Small steps are okay with me."

"Are they? Because all I want to do is to leap into the fire and damn the consequences."

His inhale was sharp.

She turned to face him. "I've never known this…wildness before, Renzo. Everything I did and didn't do, right up to what kind of man I dated and let close, it was colored by...Pia and my mom." She swallowed the knot of shame that came with the confession. "I let them live rent-free in my head, dictating my every thought and action, and that's my fault. But this...you and me... I want to act on what I want, moving forward. And that courage comes from trusting that you want this too. That you want me and that there are no twisted reasons behind it." She pushed away the sudden surge of emotion pulsing behind her confession. "You have no idea how...liberating it is. So thank you."

His gaze flashed with understanding. Covering her from prying eyes with his wide frame, he stole a hard kiss that spun her senses into liquid sensation. "Did I tell you how magnificent you are, *bella*? When you walked out of the elevator, all I wanted to do was devour you. In that, we're equals then, *sì*?"

Throat tight, she simply nodded.

As they stepped onto the dock, she straightened her shoulders. Still, nerves twisted in her stomach. With his hawklike attention, Renzo must have noticed, because he leaned closer, his voice a low murmur. "We don't have to stay long. Just tell me if it becomes too much at any point during the evening."

"No," she said, lifting her chin. "I want to meet your friends. I want to know more about your life."

"And will you share more about yours?"

She colored at his sneak attack. "You already know everything about me."

"Only what Pia told Santo and then Santo me. And we both know that's far too many filters and distortion on the way."

Biting her lower lip, she held his gaze. "I've led a very uninteresting life."

"Let me be the judge of that," the man said, relentless like a dog with a bone.

Mimi sighed. The last thing she wanted to do was to dig up the painful past. "I could be persuaded to share a few things if you kiss me like that again."

His expression softened slightly, a flicker of approval in his dark eyes. "It's a deal, *cara*."

Mimi's eyes widened as they entered the hotel, the grandeur of the lobby threatening to devour her.

It was a dazzling blend of history and modernity. Intricate Murano glass chandeliers hung from vaulted ceilings, their light reflecting off polished marble floors. Gilded mirrors lined the walls, doubling the elegance of the space.

She inhaled deeply, nerves tightening as she spotted the small crowd gathered just beyond the main reception. A hostess ushered them toward a private salon.

As the heavy double doors opened, a burst of laughter and chatter spilled into the hallway. Inside, nearly thirty people mingled, the air alive with energy and curiosity. Her pulse quickened as numerous guests turned in their direction.

This wasn't an intimate dinner with two of his closest friends.

This was...something else.

Renzo's entire body stiffened at her side. His hand fell away from her back. When she glanced up, his dark gaze was locked on the center of the room, where his sister

Chiara stood, a champagne flute in hand and a satisfied smile on her lips.

She walked up to them, impeccably dressed in a silver gown that shimmered like liquid moonlight, looking anything but repentant.

"Chiara?" Renzo muttered, his voice low and sharp. And then he switched to rapid Italian, but the gist was clear to Mimi.

He was furious with his sister. Particularly about the guests she had included, although Mimi didn't understand exactly who.

"You were taking too long, Renzo, squirrelling her away as if we might all eat her up," she said, her voice dripping with sweetness that didn't quite reach her eyes. She turned to Mimi, her smile sharpening. "You look more than fine to me, Mimi. We all began to wonder if there was a reason my brother was hiding you."

The insult and the insinuation were faultless.

Mimi forced a polite smile, though her stomach twisted. This wasn't a warm welcome—it was an ambush. As Chiara gestured toward the crowd, Mimi's gaze swept the room. Older men and women with sharp eyes and polished appearances mingled with younger women, several of whom stared at her with barely concealed amusement or disdain. At least two of the women, she guessed, had been invited because they had shown interest in Renzo at some point.

Was that why he was so angry?

It was bad enough that they all knew her through Pia and her grasping, manipulative, self-destructive ways. Now they thought Mimi had gone one step further and trapped Renzo with a pregnancy.

The media and the whole world were one thing, but facing actual people who immediately jumped to horrible conclusions about her was another. Either she ran away and let them cement those assumptions or she stayed and showed them who she was. After that, their judgment was on them.

Even two weeks ago, Mimi would have run away, would have called it his world. But now with Renzo by her side, she owed it to him and their son. And to herself.

"You had no right to do this," Renzo said to Chiara, voice clipped.

Mimi laid a hand on Renzo's arm as she felt the tension radiating from him. "It's fine," she said softly, even though her heart pounded. "I did agree to meet your friends. There are more than I expected here, that's all."

His head snapped toward her, his jaw tight. "I will not expose you to unnecessary stress."

"I can't hide forever, Renzo," she said, her voice firmer than she felt. "Plus, just because I'm averse to drama doesn't mean I'm scared of it," she said, loud enough for Chiara to hear.

The woman raised a brow, much like her brother did. The gesture was now so familiar to Mimi that the tension fled her muscles. "Let me make my own impression, Renzo. I need to do this." Pia's shadow loomed large enough without her cowering away from Renzo's family.

For a moment, he simply stared at her, the anger in his eyes warring with something softer. Finally, he gave a tight nod, though his hand slipped to her waist, pulling her closer as if shielding her from the room.

God, how her insides melted at the possessive, protective gesture. No one had ever quite looked out for her like this man did, and Mimi found new meaning in the vows they had both taken in front of these very people.

Chiara's eyes flicked to her brother's arm, her smile tightening. "Come now, don't let us keep you from the fun. Everyone's eager to meet the woman who's managed to drag Renzo to the altar."

"You have made a grave mistake, Chiara. Coming for me is one thing. Coming for Mimi…" He shook his head.

A flash of fear danced in Chiara's sparkling eyes before her mouth pursed. "You talk as if you would choose her over us, Renzo."

"It's not even a choice, because she has never embarrassed me. You have that honor, Chiara. I have repeatedly warned you that Mimi's off limits."

"Is she that fragile then?"

"If you don't respect my wife, then maybe I can wash my hands of clearing your husband's business debts, *sì*?"

CHAPTER NINE

BY THE TIME they returned to the penthouse, Renzo's mood grew darker. With a softly whispered "Need a shower," Mimi disappeared into the bathroom the moment they had stepped inside.

He couldn't blame her for not wanting to be around him.

His entire family, including his various cousins and their wives, had been out in droves, taking their cue from Chiara, ready and raring to not only judge Mimi but find her wanting. Even the polite ones. Their nod to her had been as the woman who gave birth to the new DiCarlo heir.

In contrast, his wife had been the model of elegance and grace. Never rising to the bait, smiling at a rude, intrusive comment about her pregnancy and even managing a laugh when one of his younger cousins—motivated by temperament and not intention—had asked her about how she leashed Renzo.

His father had curled his upper lip when she'd asked Massimo if he was okay. As if she was some stranger showing greedy curiosity about their family.

Massimo, at least, had the sense to ask her about one of her documentaries.

Mama, realizing how furious Renzo was, had showed her kindness by cutting through rude conversations, asking about Luca and her parents, and offering to babysit whenever they wanted alone time.

Forget alone time with him. He wouldn't be surprised if Mimi wanted to run away from the lot of them tomorrow morning.

The beautiful skyline flashed in front of his eyes, on and off, as he walked the living room like a caged animal. A wounded one at that.

How dare his sister invite Rosa, of all women? As if Renzo were still a bachelor. As if it didn't rile him up no end to see the woman who'd discarded him years ago without second glance.

What the hell had his sister thought to achieve?

He had done so much for them—for Papa and Chiara and Massimo—and never complained about it. He had had to grow up faster than any of them, make hard decisions for their family, take on the mantle of the family finances.

He had always been so proud of being the one who saved his family, who restored the respect and might to the DiCarlo name again. Somewhere along the line, it had become his identity, his ego. And yet suddenly, it felt too heavy to carry—built of others' expectations of him, of his own ambition and achievements—but also empty.

As if he had built his castle on sinking sand.

Cristo, but he missed his older brother like a hole in his chest. Santo hadn't wanted anything to do with the flaming hot mess that had been the family's company or the responsibility of bringing their father to heel. Or to deal with their younger siblings' privileged problems.

But he had been a steady, calming support behind Renzo as he took on the task of fixing the family's finances. His marriage to Pia had frustrated Renzo no end, but his brother had loved her. Had been completely loyal to her.

Had that been at the root of his resentment toward her too? That Pia had constantly needed Santo, that she took him away from Renzo and deprived him of the little he had of his brother?

Had his own anger for her been fueled by his own selfish needs?

Because Santo had been the one person who had seen beyond what Renzo could do for him.

Now Renzo wished Santo were here to help him understand the force of his anger. It wasn't like his family's shenanigans and poor impulse control were new to him. And yet it had never bothered him this much before.

They tarred Mimi with the same brush as Pia despite his vehement declaration that it wasn't true. But worse was their lack of consideration for him. Their lack of empathy or understanding for everything he had shouldered not just in the past year but for more than a decade now.

Only Mimi, even at loggerheads with him in the beginning, even as she distrusted him, had understood the rawness of his grief at losing his brother, his friend.

Hands shaking, he poured himself a finger of whiskey and downed it in one gulp. It didn't soothe him one bit. Which meant he had to leave the penthouse. He didn't want to be near her when his anger was a cold burn in his body, a sticky coating in his throat.

"Renzo?" Mimi's tentative tone came from behind him.

Whiskey sloshed over his hand as he poured himself another finger and threw that back too before he turned.

His wife stood framed by the arched doorway, hands clasped in front of her in a nervous gesture that went straight to his heart. But the rest of her...was a feast to his senses.

His erection throbbed painfully at the mere sight of her, and all he wanted was to press her against the wall and bury himself deep inside her. Work his anger and frustration and this shrapnel of hurt out on her luscious body until he could escape it all.

With emerald-green silk shorts and a camisole in the same color draped against her curves, she looked...like a delicious meal he wanted to wolf down. Her face glowed with that freshly scrubbed look. With her long, wavy hair in a braid, she was eons away from the woman who had been full of elegant grace all evening.

But just as sexy, and only his.

Suddenly, he understood another little nugget at the source of his general resentment. Something about this woman brought back all the needs and desires he'd conditioned himself to not feel. Love and affection and companionship and understanding...all things he'd been determined to not need, he wanted them now.

He grabbed his discarded jacket and held it in front of him. "You need anything?" he said brusquely.

Her gaze widened. "Don't tell me you have investor meetings at this time of the night?"

"I don't."

Her arms went around her midriff, and Renzo knew that she was bracing herself against him. "Did I say or do something wrong? At the party?" She blinked. "I mean, I know I spent too much time chatting with Massimo, but he was helping me remember all your cousins, and he's easy to talk to once you—"

Renzo cut her off. "He was good to you, then?"

"What? Yes, of course," she said, looking shocked. "He's no worse than any privileged young man, Renzo. But he's not a lost cause. At the risk of interfering in your family matter, I think he got the message this time."

"It is your family too, *bella*."

"Luca's definitely. Really, Renzo, you can't expect them all to just like me when we have six years of—"

"*You* behaved like a decent person."

"I did. But I have nothing to lose like they do."

Nothing to lose…was that how she still saw their relationship? Had she no stake in it? Renzo breathed out a rough exhale, feeling as if an invisible hand had punched him. "What the hell do they have to lose?"

Mimi sighed. "I mean, you threatened Chiara right in front of me. And all night, you hovered around me as if you were a mama bird, and—"

"I don't like that analogy one bit. Not even accurate, because the last thing I feel toward you is maternal."

She laughed then, and it took everything he had in him to not pounce on her and carry her away to the bedroom like a conquering overlord. And then he would pillage and plunder her and…get her to admit that this marriage, their relationship, was important to her. That it wasn't a level-headed transaction she could walk away from when the time was up.

"My point is…Massimo told me you haven't brought a girlfriend to any party or family function in a long time. They've not heard of you admiring a woman, even in passing."

"Because I never wanted to advertise my affairs and embarrass my family like Papa does."

"Yes. But all they see is you being so protective around me. They all feel threatened. How can you not see it? You hold their fates in your palm, and they think I'll sway your head."

"They think you're like Pia," he said, brow clearing. "They don't know that the last thing you would ever want is that kind of power over anyone. The simplest things in life are most important to you."

Her eyes widened, shimmering with a wild energy. Undeterred by his dark mood, she kept moving toward him. Bare shoulders stiff, the end of her braid dancing with her movements, eyes drinking him in. When she reached him, the scent of her soap and skin replaced the oily anger in his throat instantly. Releasing him from the coil of frustration and fury.

"Exactly," she said. "But it will take them time to see that. You can't just demand that they respect me, Renzo."

"If I can pay their kids' private school fees and support their privileged lives, then I can demand that, yes." He shook his head. "Plus, you're the mother of my child. That should automatically get you their respect." He sounded like a grumpy, arrogant, ruthless asshole like she'd called him a long time ago.

She reached him, her folded arms grazing his. "Leave it be, Renzo. At least for tonight."

His jacket slipped and fell to the floor with a silent hiss, and his breath...suspended in his throat.

Her brown eyes held his, that crystal-clear clarity he

found maddeningly arousing simmering there. She said, "I was hoping you'd stay with me tonight."

"I won't be good company, *cara*," he said, his blood heating at her nearness. "I can't be...what you need tonight."

Leaning closer, she rested her chin on his folded arms and looked up at him. "What if we don't have to talk?"

Renzo's breath left him in a shuddering exhale. He snuck his fingers under her hair, circled the fragile arc of her nape and pulled her closer. That she came without resisting, giving him her weight, made every muscle in him bunch with need. The lush curves of her breasts pressed against his chest, and he groaned.

"I don't think it's a good idea, Mimi."

She pouted, dragging his gaze to her lips. "You know, you can just say you don't want to have sex with me. I can take it."

His hand slipped down her back to her waist, and he pulled her roughly towards him. She was tall enough that his erection dragged against her belly. He felt his hips instinctually buck against the cushiony softness of her belly, seeking more.

A breathy gasp fell from her lips, her fingers locking around his neck. She pushed into his body with an eager, open abandon that made renewed heat punch through him. *Cristo*, she was going to bring him to his knees... "My control is thin tonight."

The tip of her tongue swiped over her lower lip, making it glisten. "You're distressed," she said, her gaze searching his. "About more than just their bad behavior."

"*Sì*." He scoffed. "Although *distressed* is the wrong word."

"Right," she said, opening her mouth and then closing it.

Renzo watched, fascinated by everything she did. Slowly, her shoulders straightened. "These last two months, you've been so good to me. And as your partner, I want to do something for you today. I mean, I'm cleared for everything."

"Cleared for what?" he said, doubts pricking at his throat like thorns. *Cristo*, what was wrong with him tonight?

Her throat rippled with her swallow. "Rough sex might still not be the greatest idea, but…" She opened her glistening lips in an O and made a popping sound. "I haven't gone down on a man before, but I've always been a fast learner. If you don't mind walking me through it."

If the world had turned upside down at that moment, Renzo would have been less shocked. In one swooping movement, he lifted her and perched her on top of the glass table. Then he buried his face in her neck, inhaling her scent deep into his lungs.

Emotion he didn't understand overwhelmed him.

It was both comical and touching how she wanted to soothe him, to give him an escape from reality. No one, not even his mother, had ever wondered if he needed respite and relief from all the burdens they placed on him.

Cupping her shoulders, he pulled back and considered her. Then, slowly he undid her braid, until the soft tendrils kissed her cheeks, making her look even more innocent than usual. "You thank me one moment and insult me in the next, *bella*. When did I give you the impression that I expect sexual favors for being a decent man?"

"You're more than a decent man, Renzo," she said,

pushing a lock of hair back from his forehead. He didn't miss the possessiveness in the gesture. "Also, wanting to do something good for you after everything you did for me...isn't that how we build this relationship? Beyond just loving Luca?"

Her hands stayed on him all the while, and *that* definitely soothed his raw edges. Maybe their relationship was transactional in nature at the fundamental level, but this way, they had the right expectations of each other. Maybe this was the only way their relationship could thrive and grow.

Still, it pricked him that her desire came from something so...polite and decent at the source. He wanted her as mindless with desire as he was for her.

Shifting closer to her, he spread his hands on her silky-smooth thighs. Her eyes grew wide and molten as he nudged her knees apart.

Bracing herself on her palms by her sides, she bowed her long neck then arched up to look at him. "Renzo?"

"When I said my control was thin, I didn't mean I would get rough with you physically, *bella*. I would never hurt you, Mimi."

"I know that," she said breathily.

"I meant that I'm in a devouring mood."

Her silk top pulled across her breasts, calling his attention to the tight nipples beading against it. "What do you mean?" Her breath gushed out in a pant as he swiped a knuckle over one proud peak.

Under his hand, her hip was lush and thick. He let his gaze wander over her, from her smooth golden skin to the lushness of her curves as a result of the pregnancy. Everything about her...glowed, inside and out.

And Renzo had the recurring thought that she wouldn't have crossed the orbit into his life if not for the surrogacy. Colored by his own prejudices and his ego, he would've never given her another glance. Never acknowledged the simmering connection between them.

And yet, as he looked at her now, staring up at him with achingly naked desire, sharp resentment at his own inadequacy pricked him.

She was too good for him, too smart, too self-sufficient, too...capable. That was at the root of his frustration, his anger. She made him wonder if there was anything he could offer her that would bind her to him. Other than their son.

Nor was he so full of honor that he would give her up.

"Renzo?"

"You're eager to soothe me? To talk me off the ledge of this dark mood?"

"Yes. I'll do anything."

"Then let me bury my face between your thighs and taste you."

It was the last thing Mimi had expected her brooding husband to say.

The word *husband* still tasted strange on her tongue, but she was beginning to like it more every day. And tonight, at the party, she had a true taste of what it was to have a man like Renzo DiCarlo be her husband in the real sense.

A partner, a protector, a caregiver, and a fierce ally if someone else came for her, even if that was his family.

Cracks had splintered in the hard shell she'd built around her heart. Suddenly she felt helpless against all the longings he set loose inside her. With each sly comment and innuendo-riddled glance, Mimi had only found herself growing stronger.

With Renzo by her side, no one could touch her. But she also realized that they were curious about not just her or Luca, but the hold she had on her powerful husband.

True to the vow he'd made to her at their wedding ceremony, despite her own reluctance to be a part of it, Renzo had kept every word.

With each brush of his body against her, with each little touch—his hand on her lower back, his arm around her waist, his fingers dancing over her nape—she'd found herself falling deeper and deeper into her own desire.

"Do you want to go into the bedroom?" she asked, sounding like a frightened virgin. Which she was not. But from the first moment she had laid eyes on him years ago, Renzo made her feel defensive. Even now, he provoked the wildness inside her, pushing her to prove something to him. And to herself.

Or was it that he made her feel so safe that she could let out all the desires and wants she'd buried deep beneath rationale? Was it her trust in him that she'd never known with any other man that made her not want to back down?

Renzo's smirk was full of devilish teasing. "No, *bella*. Unless you're shy about these things and want the cover of darkness?"

This was what he meant when he said his control was thin tonight. He meant to demand her surrender in a way she'd never given any man. "I'm not…a virgin," Mimi said, full-on blushing now. She needed to get this out, though. "But I don't have a lot of experience. I mean…"

"I guess we could do this under the covers then."

Something dark danced in Renzo's eyes, and every inch of her trembled in response. "It's not what I want for tonight, but I guess I shall make do."

She bristled and straightened her shoulders. "You're pushing me, knowing how much I hate to look incompetent."

He laughed then, and it was full of a...strange emotion she seemed to provoke in him. A shiver zinged down her spine as she wondered if it could be fondness or even affection. "Competence has nothing to do with this, Mimi."

His hands danced on the band of her silk shorts, pulling at the soft elastic and then letting it go, so that it snapped over and over. And then, in that little gap between, he brushed his fingers over her skin. Going a sliver lower each time.

Such fleeting contact, and yet she felt it as if he were branding her with a hot poker. The tips of his fingers could be leaving scorch marks on her flesh for how seared she felt.

Slowly, fisting her fingers tight in his shirt, Mimi pushed herself back. The muscles in her belly strained, but she kept going.

Dark, hungry eyes watched every movement, and she wondered if this was their own version of a trust fall. She had no doubt that he was testing her and expecting, almost wanting, her to fail. The latter she didn't understand.

So that he could refuse her invitation without offending her? Or because, for once in her life, Renzo needed someone else, and he couldn't bear it? Did he need her as much as she needed him?

Finally, her elbows bumped into the glass table behind her. Holding his gaze, she let her head fall back all the way too.

Her front felt like it was on fire while the cool glass kissed her back. Renzo's hand moved to her upper thighs, and she spread them like he told her to. "I never back down from a challenge."

Everything in her protested at how she was spread out before him. And yet for Renzo, she wanted to do this.

The light from the chandelier was bright against her eyes, hiding his shadowed expression from her. Instead, she looked down over her own body. Her nipples stood out hard and throbbing, while her silk top pulled up, baring a silky swath of her midriff.

"Plant your feet on the armrests of the chair."

Mimi bit back the automatic protest that rose to her lips. She would be completely open to his gaze like that. Something about his stance told her he was waiting for her to back down, to walk away from him in his dark mood. To play it safe and by the rules. Stay between the lines that Pia and her mother had drawn for her, like she'd always done all her life.

He wanted her to prove to him, and herself, that she could be what he wanted, or needed, at a time like this.

That little wildness she'd always caged inside her, afraid of failing measured against her mother and her stepsister, fluttered its wings against the bars. She planted her feet firmly and made sure to dig her toes into his hard thighs.

Renzo's hands lingered on the seam of her shorts. Then in one swoop, he pulled them off.

Mimi didn't want to think too much about how smooth

his actions were. After the clunky, unsatisfactory attempts at sex, she wanted a partner who actually knew what to do.

She wanted Renzo's confidence and his skill to undo her as his eyes had been promising from day one. But she was also afraid of the aftermath. Of how he would change her, because nothing in her life had prepared her for a man like him.

She barely processed the cool sensation of the glass against her buttocks when his fingers delved into her core. Sensation skewered her. His fingers were cold, the tips rough against her intimate folds. His movements, though...were gentle and slow, not lingering long enough at any one spot.

That small ache she had been feeling all evening, for days even, flared into an impossible flame, begging to be put out. Panting, already writhing, she bit her lower lip to keep any sound from escaping.

And those eyes of his...they held her in a challenge, in a thrall. Even as his wicked fingers learned every inch of her.

A soft mewl escaped her anyway when he dipped the tip of one finger into her slit. The mindless way he dipped and drew back tightened her belly muscles like they were taut springs. "*Dio mio*, all this for me, *bella*?"

"Yes," she said in a near shout, every inch of her protesting when his fingers retreated. "It's for you, Renzo. If you're forgetting how we got here—" her voice was a ragged whisper "—it's because I've thrown myself at you, okay? I'm horny for you. I sniff at your shirts like an addict. I rub your body wash over my body because I like the smell of you on my skin. I...sneak glances at you when you return from the gym downstairs, dripping in sweat, because your body turns me on. Everything about you, the way you look at me, the way you look after me, the way you..." Her breath hitched. "Everything turns me on, and I've never felt this way."

He chuckled, but the sound was hollow. Even self-deprecating, while the hunger in his eyes dialed up to devouring. "You don't have to sneak glances at me, *bella*. I'm all yours."

"You say that and yet you..." Whatever else she had been about to say floated away as he bent his head and his tongue unnervingly found her clit, as if she'd given him a hand-drawn map.

Mimi jerked, her spine arching into his touch as if she were a puppet and he held her strings. Not that she cared one bit. He could turn her inside out if he touched her like this.

She barely processed the first lazy, languorous stroke when he changed it up to little circles. On and on, over and over, he tapped, licked and stroked at her clit while his fingers brushed in and out of her, going deeper every time.

The pleasure coiled, intense, breath-stealing, spiraling, and Mimi buried her hands in his hair, both terrified and excited.

When he stopped licking and instead sucked at her with those sinuous lips that she couldn't get over kissing, with a scandalous, erotic sound, she went off.

Her orgasm crashed through her, shaking her from within, thrashing her around, making her shiver from head to toe. A moan slipped from her as she caught the sight of her husband's arrogant head squeezed between her trembling thighs.

With a smacking kiss on her outer lips, Renzo looked

up. Lips damp with her arousal, hair mussed by her hands, and a wicked smile bringing out all those little imperfections that she adored so much…her heart gave a jarring thud against her chest, and her channel fluttered.

The orgasm should have wiped her out, and yet she felt achingly empty. Voraciously hungry for more. He hadn't fully penetrated her, and suddenly she was obsessed with knowing how he would feel inside her.

She tried to push up, but her body was mostly made of pudding right then.

Pulling back from the cradle of her thighs, Renzo adjusted her shorts and then gave her a hand. A sudden shyness engulfed her as she took it, her eyes level with his. "That was…" she started, then stopped. "Do you want that review now?"

"Not really," he said, patting her cheek. She could smell her arousal on his fingers, and that did strange, wicked things to her insides. "The sounds you make when you come apart are mine and only mine, *si*? That's reward enough."

She grasped his palm and brought those very fingers to her lips. She wanted to shock him like he had done her. But even more than that, she wanted to let her deepest, darkest desires out to play. What better man than Renzo DiCarlo, her husband by law, to indulge herself with?

She could live a hundred lives, and he would still be the man she would trust to not mock her or belittle her or wish she was someone she wasn't and never could be. Opening her mouth, she licked at the tips of his fingers before sucking one inside her mouth.

His sharp exhale was all the encouragement she needed. Wrapping her tongue around the digit, she sucked at his long finger. His jaw tightened, and a curse fell from his lips. Then she released him with a popping sound. "Now, am I allowed to devour you too? Or are you one of those men who demand surrender from their partner but can't give an inch?"

CHAPTER TEN

THE BREATH PUNCHED out of Renzo at his wife's pure challenge. With her tart taste still on his tongue, her lush body in his hands, he felt giddy as if he had drunk way too much. Which he never had, even as a young adult.

Because he'd had to be the responsible one.

Suddenly, strong arms and soft curves wound around him in that sweet torment. "Come back to me, Renzo."

He sank his fingers into her hair, his willpower in shreds.

Cristo, he wanted to own this woman so badly that he was shaking with it. But it was more than just simple lust.

It was the way she challenged him, sought to understand him, saw him as more than the ruthless, powerful billionaire who could give her whatever she wanted. And now this...passionate, bold creature met his gaze with a tilted chin and glistening lips.

"I'm afraid your hand or your mouth would not do tonight, *cara*. I want to be inside you. And I want to know how you feel when you fight it so much, as if you have to earn the pleasure, and then inevitably fall apart."

Color streaked her cheeks, and damn if it didn't get him all hot and hard. Then her eyes widened, as if with dawning realization. "I mean, I have never...so hard that

I nearly blacked out, but I thought that was just how I was…"

He liked that she was shy about sex and intimacy and yet bold enough to come to him. To admit to wanting to devour him. To reveal that she wanted him so much that all those little inhibitions fell away.

Now he realized what it had cost her to not only come to him but to offer to soothe him in any way he liked. It wasn't simply a sexual favor she'd offered but her trust, her hope that she could make a difference in his mood.

He clasped her cheek and took her mouth in a soft kiss. She tasted of her own arousal and something fundamentally her. A taste he couldn't define but already knew he would never get enough of.

They surfaced from the kiss, arms tangled around each other, their breaths harsh, the tips of their noses touching. Renzo rubbed his fingers over her lower lip, incapable of not touching her even in that state. "I mean, I will make do with your hand, *bella*," he whispered at her temple, then slid his mouth to the delicate shell of her ear, "if it's too much. I don't want to hurt you or cause you discomfort."

"I will tell you if it gets…" she blushed again. "The only thing the doctor warned against was to not feel forced emotionally. I told her that wasn't a worry with us. And then I embarrassed her by admitting that I probably would have to seduce you. I also had an IUD put in. I'm allergic to latex."

As always, her efficient response both startled and fascinated him. And aroused him no end.

Renzo scooped her off the table. With a squeal, she wrapped her arms and legs around him and buried her face in his neck. The rough strokes of her exhales, the press of her breasts against his chest, the drag of her belly against his cock made his skin burn with need.

He dropped her onto the bed and instantly crawled over her, straddling her hips. The gold highlights in her brown hair glinted in the light. Hair spread like a halo around his pillow, breasts rising and falling, she looked… enchantingly beautiful.

But it was the trust in her eyes, the absolute naked need for him, that made her a goddess in his own.

Pushing her knees apart, he let his lower body press hers into the bed. Her thighs fell away on a breathless gasp, and the heat and dampness of her core seeped into his trousers.

Her hips thrust up in a quick tilt just as he canted his own down. Their groans rent the air, joining in a rough melody. "That…feels amazing," she said, a dizzy smile curving her lips. "Please. I want to feel more of you. I want…" again that lip-bite as if she was giving away too much "…all of you."

"Not yet," he whispered, swatting away her hands when they moved to his abdomen. "You tormented me for weeks, your hands all over me, your curves pressed against me. I mean to avenge myself, *bella*. Plus, there's too much of you I haven't kissed or touched or licked yet."

He laughed when she pouted and took her in a rough kiss she met with equal ferocity. They licked and nipped at each other, their teeth clanking in a fierce duel.

Then he filled his hands with her smooth skin and lush curves.

The thrust of her clavicle to her shoulders, to the smooth skin between her breasts and then to the lush mounds that filled his hands to overflowing…he rolled the hem of her silk top up and kissed the undersides of her breasts. And when the fabric got into his way too much, he grabbed it with both hands and ripped it apart.

Her breasts fell into his waiting hands. Eyes closed, Mimi arched into his touch as he kneaded them and then kissed around the aureoles, taking his time.

He continued, never touching the aching buds with his fingers or lips. Slender fingers dove into his hair with a rough grasp and pulled. "Please Renzo. No more teasing."

Just as he was about to lick the hard peaks, a drop of milk appeared.

Mimi stiffened instantly, embarrassed color pouring into her cheeks like hot lava. One slim hand came to cover up her breast. "I pumped before the shower, but—"

Renzo gently pushed her hand aside and licked up the stray drop. It was sweet on his tongue. "Don't tell me you're ashamed of something your body does to nurture our son, Mimi. I thought you too sensible for that."

"Not ashamed." She licked at the beads of sweat dotting her upper lip. "All this, you, it's too raw, too much sometimes. It almost feels like I'll drown in all that you make me feel, Renzo. And that I'm alone with it."

"You are not," Renzo said before finding her mouth.

Mimi sank into his kiss, as if his assurance was a vow. Her hands moved over his back, and she tugged at his shirt. "Want to feel your skin."

"My wife's wish is my command," he said, pushing to his knees.

Wide eyes took him in as he shed the shirt first. He undid the fly of his trousers and waited. That blush he adored stole up her neck and cheeks before she said, "Yes, please. All of you."

Renzo kicked off his trousers and boxers in one sweep. Her gaze skidded over every inch of him, never staying, never lingering. And his skin burned at the intensity of her openly greedy perusal.

Pushing up gently, breasts heaving, she raked a nail down his nipple, then followed the thick trail of hair down past his abdomen and stopped. "You're beautiful," she whispered.

"Lie back and touch me," Renzo said, straddling her hips.

She licked her lips in that nervous gesture of hers, but the way her fingers flexed and grasped his cock was firm. A soft gasp huffed out of her. "God, I can't wait to feel you inside me."

He threw his head back and exhaled, fighting the ravenous urge to pump into her hand. But he was too greedy for the sight of her like this—sprawled over his bed, deliciously naked and spread out for him, and her slender fingers fisting him tight—to look away for too long.

And just as he imagined, her brow was tight in concentration, lower lip caught between her teeth. "Keep squeezing me, Mimi. As hard as you can." Already he was panting, his control nearly nonexistent around her.

If she applied herself a little more rigorously—which, knowing her, he knew she would—he was going to spill all over her lush breasts and thick belly.

Like he had promised her, like they had been both waiting for apparently for some time now, he wanted to be inside her. He wanted to make her his wife completely, tonight. Now.

Which meant he wanted her to fall over with him, one

more time. He wanted to feel her channel flutter and fall apart around him.

Leaning forward, keeping his full weight off her, he kissed her mouth softly. Instantly, her grip on his cock released, her fingers moving to his nape. She moaned and writhed under him, trapping his erection against her belly.

"I love the taste of you everywhere, *bella*," he whispered, licking the long line of her neck, kissing a trail between her breasts. He made a stop and teased her nipples into hard peaks again with his lips and tongue.

On and on, he went on a journey of discovery down her body. Every little patch of her skin, every little divot and crease and fold, he tasted all of her. Left his own marks. Claimed every inch of her.

Her breathing shallowed, her body undulating like a cresting wave under his caresses as he built her toward the peak again.

His name was a chant, falling over and over from her lips as he played with her clit and folds again. Wetness coated his fingers, and he smeared it all over her folds.

"Tell me anytime if it becomes too much," he whispered, pressing his forehead to hers, gritting his teeth, nudging the head of his cock against her slit, "and I'll stop."

A soft sob broke through her lips as he pushed the broad head in. Her fingers clasped his biceps, nails digging into him. Her gaze, though, clear and certain as always, held his. "More, Renzo. Please, I'm dying of anticipation here."

He chuckled and pressed in a little more. "You're tight, *bella*, and resisting me. Always resisting me," he said, kissing her temple. "Relax for me."

Her spine arched into him, and her feet came to rest on his buttocks. "I just... I want this to be good for you, Renzo."

"If it got any better, I would probably expire," he said, and thrust in all the way.

She jerked and stilled.

Sweat dripping from his forehead, Renzo sought her mouth again. He kissed her hard, all the tension in him rippling out into the kiss. She let him ravage her, giving it back in equal measure. "Tell me, Mimi. Tell me how it feels."

"Full and achy and not enough." Her brown eyes held a spark of mischief that sent heat to his balls. "Whatever you're doing, it's not enough, Renzo. I need more. I need..." that pretty pink blush stole into her cheeks as she dragged her nails down his back and onto his buttocks "...faster and harder. And I want to come again."

"Yes to everything, *bella*," he said, pulling her hips up and canting his down at the same time. This time when he stroked into her, the movement dragged against her popped clit.

She reacted instantly, her pelvis muscles choking him and clasping him harder and harder.

He took her in long, deep strokes but at a slow pace that he thought might kill him soon. "I'm close, *cara*. And you squeeze me so well that I can't stop myself. Touch yourself. Get yourself to the edge."

Eyes wide as pools, the tip of her tongue peeking out, she ran her hand down between their bodies. The tentative graze of her fingers against the root of his shaft drove him wild, relentless heat running down his spine.

Their gazes dove down their bodies to where they were joined, and then sought each other.

Her soft cries added to the rough symphony of their bodies coming together and pulling apart. Leaning down, Renzo caught her nipple between his lips and gave a rough tug.

Instantly, she shattered around him, her muscles milking him for all he was worth.

His own release thundered down on him, and he pumped his hips wildly, eager to ride the wave, roughly using up her delicate flesh.

The intensity of it doubled when Mimi arched up and reached for his mouth. She took him on another ride with a rough, greedy, grasping kiss. Damp eyes full of wonder and trust clung to his as if she hadn't expected it to be this good. As if she had needed this more than she needed her breath.

As if nothing existed for her except him and this feverish intimacy between them.

He was the one who wanted to own her, who had his name falling from her lips like a chant. Yet strangely, Renzo felt owned by his wife, like no one had ever owned him.

Mimi ran her hand over Renzo's forearm, relishing the solid feel of him under her fingers. Her body was still humming from the aftershocks of their frenzy, and her heart felt like it had grown too big for her chest and was dancing a jig.

She might have guessed that sex with her husband might be a soul-wrenching experience that would change her composition, as it were. Already, she felt freer and bolder and easier in her body than she had ever felt. And more confused, more possessive and more selfish too.

She grimaced as she moved her legs to scissor through Renzo's, and her core twitched with soreness.

With his powerful body draped over her from behind, she felt...protected. It was an alien thing to her, and she didn't know how to feel about the emotion itself.

If she wasn't careful, she might even end up craving it. And yet was it so wrong, so selfish, to want this intimacy with him after a round of such passionate sex?

"You're in pain?" Renzo said, stiffening behind her. "I've hurt you."

Mimi tightened her grip over him, loath to lose the cocoon of his body. She didn't want to move from the bed or face all the feelings she'd have to process the moment they stepped out of it. "If you get out of this bed, I will be very mad, Renzo."

She felt his tension releasing a little. His breath danced over her nape. "Tell me how you feel."

His command would have grated on her any other time. But now she could hear the undercurrent of his uncertainty, of his dark mood still hovering over them like a black cloud. And that earlier urge to soothe him, to share whatever it was that bothered him, was magnified by a hundred times. "Like I've had two mind-blowing orgasms. Like I've satisfied my very sexy, very studly Italian husband with my body. Like I've been remade." She couldn't help giggling at the last.

"Mimi..." he said, his voice far too grave.

Mimi frowned, and as if to soothe herself, she pulled his hand up to her face and kissed the center. The shape of his fingers, the lines on his palm, the rough mound of his hand...when had he grown so familiar to her?

She couldn't get over the plain fact that she could touch Renzo DiCarlo like this. Freely. Whenever she wanted.

"It was quite the workout, Renzo. And while I've been slowly getting back to walking and other forms of exercise, this was a lot of...rigor." She laughed at her own word choice, hoping he would join in too. No such luck though. "Of course I'm sore. And no, you didn't hurt me. At all."

The press of his lips over her upper back made her shiver. As did his broad hand cupping her hip in a possessive grip. As did the outline of his already hard shaft pressing against her bottom. "If you want to go again, my earlier offer stands," she said, making a popping sound with her mouth.

"No more tonight, *cara*," he said, nudging closer to her.

"Let me turn," she said sharply, having had enough. With a sigh, he loosened the fortress he made around her with his arms and legs.

A buffet of tiny twitches and pains greeted her as she turned to face him. His arm came to rest on her waist loosely as he studied her. She studied him in return, awed yet again that this...wonderful man was hers, in that moment at least.

His stylishly cut hair stood in all directions, his thin lips were swollen from her nips and bites, and there were scratch marks on his shoulders and chest.

He looked like he was...hers. Only hers.

And then it swept through her, like a storm ravaging a town.

Renzo DiCarlo was more than just his wealth or his

power or his arrogance. There was a wealth of goodness and caring beneath the facade he showed the world. A man capable of feeling deep emotions and deeper pain.

He had been hurt tonight by his family's boorish behavior. He had been furious on her behalf, even though she had held her own. He had made her feel so protected that just having him by her side had made her strong. Bold. She had stood up for herself, something she'd never done, not even with her own family.

And she had seen the very same loneliness in his eyes that she had known for so long. But together, they could be so much more than what they were alone.

And if she was willing to take the risk with her own heart, if she could trust him and trust herself to get this right, they could have something real. Something Mimi had never thought possible for her.

Something like...true love.

A pained gasp escaped her as she realized that she was retrofitting rationale and good sense to something that was already out of her hands. Trying to exert control over a situation when it was too late...

She was in love with her husband. Irrevocably. Completely. Like a steel fist clutching her heart in its grip. The knowledge of her love for him filled her bone and sinew, truly remaking her now.

How could she not love him when he had helped her see who she could be when she was wholly herself? When she didn't doubt her own self-worth? When she simply let herself be?

"That is my least favorite sound in the world."

His caustic tone brought Mimi back to the present, to the reality of him. To the clawing, painful truth of loving him and knowing that he might never love her in return. That had been their agreement, hadn't it?

Neither of us wants anything to do with love, he'd said when he'd proposed marriage to her. More than once he'd made it clear that the thing he admired about her was that her head and her heart were firmly planted on cold, hard ground.

"I'll check with my database and try not to produce any sounds that might offend my lordly husband," she said, her response tart and sharp, as if it could stop her love from flashing across her face like a neon sign.

God, could he see in her face how hopelessly in love she was with him? Would he mock her, cut their deal short?

His chuckle brought her gaze to his mouth. She sighed. When he laughed like that, her entire being seemed to light up as if that laugh was powering every cell.

"I do not like it when you hide yourself away, *cara*. When you're sad. I take my duties very seriously."

She knew that much about him for sure. "I'm not sad," she said morosely.

Fingers clasped her cheek, and he tilted her face this way and that as if he were searching for the truth. Throwing an arm around his neck, she pressed herself to him, her face landing in the hollow of his throat.

Joy and fear duked it out inside her, and she trembled from the effort of struggling with both. The drag of her bare breasts against his chest, though…pure, glorious sensation. She anchored herself to it.

"You're trembling, Mimi," he said, lifting her chin.

Like a wanton creature in heat, she rubbed herself against him from head to toe, hoping to distract him.

Hoping to drown herself in so much sensation that she could escape the truth sitting on her chest like an anvil.

He caught her lips with a rumbling groan that she swallowed happily. But contrary man that he was, he didn't let her deepen the kiss. Didn't let her give in to the frenzy. And she didn't have the confidence yet to push him into his own.

It was a soft kiss. Almost an apology of sorts. Something else too, something deeper that she wished he would put into words. And it nearly broke her resolve to keep the admission that burned on her lips to herself.

When he released her, she clung to him. Her mind whirred in a thousand directions. Luca was going to come home soon. And from everything she had learned about her husband so far, their bond with Luca would only deepen their bond with each other.

And yet she knew nothing about why he was so against love. Was it having been exposed to his father's constant infidelity growing up? Then there had been Pia and Santo's marriage—another disaster.

He had been upset with his family earlier tonight, but the emotion beneath had been a pulsing anger. Even hurt.

"That woman Chiara invited tonight... Rosa, I think," Mimi mumbled, impressions from the evening coming back to her now.

Instantly, Renzo tensed. "What about her?"

Mimi pulled back casually, though she kept her cheek on his arm.

"You could barely stand to look at her."

"You read me well, *cara*." He turned to lie on his back, though one arm stayed wrapped around her. "I *couldn't* stand to look at her."

"May I ask why?"

"Rosa was my best friend once. My first lover. The woman I loved. The woman I thought I would marry and build a family with." There was no bitterness in his words anymore, though. Only a strange resignation, even emptiness.

"Oh," Mimi said, as if the one word could convey her quaking insides. Clawing fingers of jealousy gripped her. The sensation was so alien to her that she rubbed a hand over her chest.

And then she remembered what she had just said. Renzo hadn't even looked in this woman's direction. He hadn't left her side even for a minute. He was nothing like his father, she reminded herself.

And yet it was his highly developed sense of duty, his version of honor that would forbid him from even looking at the woman when he was married. Didn't matter if his feelings had been revived for her or not.

"I'm sorry I asked about her then," she said, trying so hard to not probe further.

"Don't be. Your curiosity is natural. She's Chiara's close friend. She got divorced a couple of years ago. My sister's been trying to set us up again."

"And she invited her tonight even though you're now married and have a son," Mimi said, her own fury creeping into her words. It was one thing for his sister to tell Mimi that she didn't like her. A whole other to ambush him by inviting the girl he'd loved once. "And Chiara dared to call Pia manipulative."

As fast as it came, her fury tapped out, leaving her with more questions. To hell with Chiara. All she wanted to know was why Renzo had been so angry at the sight of that girl.

She scooted up into a sitting position and dragged the duvet to her chest, suddenly feeling far too restless. Damn her sister-in-law for ruining her first post-orgasmic haze with her husband.

Renzo followed her, his movements far more graceful than her jerky lumbering. "It will not happen again."

"I'm angrier on your behalf than mine." Mimi bit her lip, hating that she needed to ask the question. That she needed to know beyond doubt if he had any remnant affection for Rosa. "I… Did you consider getting back with her, Renzo, before Luca and I ruined your plans?"

Dark anger flashed in Renzo's eyes as he turned to face her. Even amid the muddle of her thoughts, Mimi couldn't not notice the sculpted musculature of his chest. Or how his olive skin gleamed and rippled when he moved.

God, she wanted to worship him with her lips and tongue and fingers and all of her. She wanted to whisper her admission of love into every sinew and bone, until he was overflowing with it.

"You are asking the wrong question, *cara*."

The darkness remained in his gaze as she hurriedly pulled up hers. Though the anger transformed to a self-satisfied smirk. "You don't have to preen that I'm drooling over you, Renzo. This is the first time in my life that I'm so completely and utterly…horny over a man. Give me a break."

Grabbing the duvet toga-style, she tried to get off the bed when instead she found herself in his lap, his arm a steel band under her breasts. She squirmed, felt his hardness poke at her behind, heard his near-pained grunt and settled in with a huff.

"Stop moving, *bella*." His desire colored his words with rich texture.

Sinking into him, she thought back to his comment. Past the new current of anxiety and awareness in her belly that reminded her she was so vulnerable against him now. *Wrong question*, he'd said... "Why did you and Rosa break up?"

He chuckled softly at her ear. The sound traveled through her, settling deep into her core, planting roots. "Have I ever told you that I find your mind as arousing as your body?"

Mimi turned, kissed him and mumbled, "No. Tell me, please. I will never mention her again."

He dipped his head until his chin rested on her shoulder. "When I was twenty-one, it came out that our family was in massive debt. The business was crumbling. Investors were pulling out. My father, whether through sheer stupidity or negligence, ran everything to ground. Rosa's father found out and told her. She sent me a message through her brother that she was canceling our engagement."

Mimi turned in his arms again and pressed her cheek to his bare chest. His heart thudded under her ears in a steady beat while hers...ached for him. No wonder he'd been so predisposed to dislike Pia too. While her sister hadn't worshipped status and wealth particularly, she had cared about the superficial stuff more than her own or Santo's happiness. "I'm sorry."

"Don't be. Rosa taught me a valuable lesson I never forgot, motivated me enough to clean up my father's mess.

It took me more than a decade, but I fixed everything. Rebuilt the resorts into a luxury brand."

"I don't understand it," Mimi said, her confusion seeping into her words. "From what Massimo told me at the party, it seems Rosa's and Chiara's husbands went into business together, and it all sank. You literally had to rescue your brother-in-law. Weren't you at least a little happy to have her see you like this? To rub your success and power and wealth in her snotty face?"

He laughed so hard that Mimi shook along with him. "What a bloodthirsty little heart you have, *cara*. I like you more and more."

Mimi shrugged, even as every inch of her thrummed at his praise. At the glint of admiration in his tone. "Instead, you were...distressed to see her. You're sure you have no lingering feelings for her?"

His teeth bit down on her earlobe, sending a lick of flaming sensation down to her sensitized core. Mimi gasped and writhed in his lap as he followed it up by licking at the hurt he caused.

"No feelings for her, *cara*. I will not have you doubt my word or my commitment to this."

"I don't, Renzo," she said, mouth falling open in a long gravelly moan as he cupped her breasts. "But I—"

She never got to finish her thought or the sentence as he spread her thighs wide open on his lap and dipped his fingers into her core.

"The way you're dripping, I'm not sure this can be termed as punishment, Mimi." One swipe of a long finger followed, from her clit to slit, and Mimi sobbed at the sharp avalanche of sensations pooling there. This time, his teeth dug into her shoulder. "Maybe I should stop."

"Please don't," she said, grasping his wrist, making his palm fall flat against her mound.

"Then we're agreed that there will be no discussion about that woman?"

Mimi knew, in the back recesses of her mind where a figment of rationale persisted, that he wasn't answering her question. That he was seducing her into forgetting the small niggling doubt she had raised.

But, God, she was helpless against his voice, against him, against the skillful strokes of his fingers. Against loving him so completely that all she wanted was the moment to go on forever.

His fingers pulled away with a tap against her clit that had her angling her hips into his hand. "I didn't hear your answer, Mimi."

"No talking about her ever again," Mimi whispered, falling back against him. Every cell in her, every inch of her being seemed to dwell at the point where he stroked her again. In clever, mindful circles that drove her out of her skin. So skilled already at what would push her to the edge.

Her climax shimmered out of reach, teasing her, taunting her. "I don't know if I can, Renzo."

"Yes, *bella*, you can. Your body sings for me, Mimi. Do you know what a turn-on that is? Do you know what it does to me when you don't hide your desire for me? When you respond to my every touch like you were the most sensitive instrument ever crafted?"

With each searing word, he played her like a maestro. And Mimi followed him up the spiraling steps, her mind, her body, her soul all his to control.

His to protect.

His to…love. If only he wanted to.

Raking her fingers through his hair, she sobbed at the intrusive thought. Reality ruining her jagged climb toward completion. "More, Renzo. Please."

He gave her everything she begged for and more. A heady cocktail of sweat and sex filled her nostrils. "Come for me, *bella*. Because then, I'm going to take you up on your offer and use your hands. Right on this bed. You'll be too sore for the rest of the night, *si*? So maybe I'll paint your breasts with my—"

Mimi clutched his wrist, arched up and off him like a bowstring pulled taut, and shattered into a thousand fragments of nothingness. And the man she utterly adored held her through it, praising her, soothing her comedown, kissing her.

As if she were precious to him too. As if she were the woman he had chosen for himself and not by a cruel twist of fate.

CHAPTER ELEVEN

Luca came home the next day while Renzo was out of town.

He had been gone the next morning when she'd woken up in their bed. A scribbled note lay fluttering on the nightstand in his quite illegible scrawl.

Urgent, unavoidable issues at ski resort at the Alps.
—R.

Nothing about when he would return or that he would miss her and their son.

Okay, yes, they weren't teenagers trading secret love notes in the classroom, but still…her foolish heart ached for something more personal.

Especially after the night they had shared, after he had so thoroughly debauched her. He had been insatiable even at dawn, waking her up to ask her if her mouth was still on offer. Of course she had whispered yes. What followed had been both revelatory of her own sexual boundaries and how easily she could cross them for him, and how savage her love for him could be. That session had ended with his powerful body shaking, praising her for her "competence" yet again.

It had nearly crushed her to wake up alone in the large bed. To find her body sore and exhausted in the best way, but to be unable to reach over and kiss him. To be unable to see the man she had fallen in love with, in the bright, fresh light of the morning with this new, keen awareness.

Tears smarting the back of her eyes, she had gotten ready for her day. When she arrived at the clinic, the neonatal specialist had informed her that she could take Luca home immediately.

A cheerful Massimo and their mother had arrived within minutes of her calling.

Mimi knew she could have waited for Renzo to return. But coward that she was, she was trying to escape all the feelings her husband evoked in her by drowning herself in her son.

Or maybe it wasn't cowardice but stubborn self-preservation. She needed to prove to herself that one passionate night with her husband hadn't rendered her foolish or incapable of doing what needed to be done. That her mind, her very nature, hadn't been rewritten by Renzo's passion for her.

Passion, not love, she reminded herself.

They had been waiting for so long for Luca to come home. Her precious baby boy was the reason she and Renzo were even together.

So she brought him home, aided by Renzo's mother, his brother, and an army of nurses and nannies that Renzo had already hired.

He had married her precisely because she was no-nonsense, capable and didn't believe in love. He had shown her immense kindness and comfort and even passion precisely because he expected her to not turn into this…lovesick, maudlin creature.

And really, what was even the guarantee that all these strange new feelings wouldn't set her up for more heartache? More rejection? And God, she had had enough to last a lifetime at her mom's hands.

So she would not change herself one bit, she told herself, burying her face into her son's belly. She would not let this love she felt for her husband make a fool out of her.

If her tears leaked out and she had to change Luca's onesie, she pretended like they were tears of happiness at his coming home.

Renzo crept into his bedroom on soft feet, moonlight his only aid in the dark room. He felt like a thief sneaking into someone else's house under the cover of night.

Frustration and anger at himself coiled like twin ropes inside him, driving the breath out of him. He saw only now that it was the intensity of his feelings for Mimi that had driven him away, causing him to miss his son being discharged from the hospital. He had been gone for two days, and it felt like two eternities.

His heart scuttled into his throat like a crab on sand as he reached the foot of the large bed.

A soft night-light had been left on his side of the bed, casting an ethereal glow. The sight that greeted him made his heart fall back into his chest with a thud.

Luca was fast asleep, cocooned tightly in a blue blanket, tiny fisted hands thrown above him as if in a cheer. Wisps of jet-black hair fluttered beneath a woolen cap, the jut of his straight nose prominent in his chubby face.

Next to Luca, with the tips of her fingers grazing his

belly, as if she couldn't bear to not touch him, was his wife. Lying on her side, with her head tucked on her folded arm. It struck Renzo that she was just as pure of heart as their son.

Two innocent, bright-as-sun lives that had come into his orbit by sheer chance. Taunting him with the fact that he hadn't even known he would want this in his life.

Leaning over, he brushed a wavy lock of hair from her face, wishing she would wake. And set those perceptive eyes on him, maybe challenge him as to why he had fled like that. Even help him figure out this confused tangle of emotions within him.

Because he *had* run away, like a coward.

After using her all night, after slaking his desire on her still-recovering body over and over.

Cristo, he hadn't expected to lose himself in her like that. Hadn't expected to find both his salvation and his destruction in her soft smiles, in her hard kisses and her willing, warm body.

But then, he shouldn't have been surprised that Mimi would be as giving and passionate in bed as she was anywhere else. Her passion had been a demanding sword and a comforting embrace all at once. He had been so out of control, so needy that he had even woken her up at dawn, demanding she give him her mouth.

But he refused to regret it. She would hate him if he regretted it because she had met him as an equal. Then he had woken up in the morning, tangled in her arms.

Bright sunlight had streamed into the room, lighting up the dark shadows under her eyes and all the marks he had left on her neck and chest. He had realized then what had disturbed him so about seeing Rosa the previous night.

His real trajectory in life had begun with her rejecting a future with him, rejecting his love.

It had become his identity—to be the provider of all things for the people around him. If he hadn't stepped up all those years ago and fixed their crumbling finances, none of them would live in the easy luxury they did now.

But in the long slog he'd put in for years, in his refusal to stop even a day for his own rest or recreation, he had become only that—a man who fixed things for others. A man whose only value lay in his wealth, in his power and reach. A man who didn't want or understand deeper connections.

He was surrounded by people who needed things from him. His beautiful, bright, brave wife had stood out in sharp contrast at that damned party for one very particular reason. A reason that stole the ground from under his feet.

What was it that Mimi needed from him? What could he give her that she would willingly bind herself to him forever?

It had been arrogant of him to assume that he would simply keep her. Because now, he wanted her to want this life with him.

If their frenzied night of lovemaking had clarified one thing, it was that he was falling for her and this little family they were building. And that he didn't have anything to offer to make her stay.

She had been reluctant about marrying him, had only given in because he'd forced her into understanding the reality of carrying his son. He hadn't exaggerated.

She and Luca did need his protection. But soon, the media's interest in them would fade, and the year would be up.

The prospect of letting her go, of learning that there was nothing he could give her to bind her to him when that day dawned...nearly brought him to his knees.

So he had gone away, using the problems with the ski resort as the perfect excuse. To think and strategize and plan, though he was realizing that there was no blueprint for this. All he could do was stall and arrest the complete descent.

Moving slowly, he climbed into the bed on the other side of his son and carefully touched his cheek with the tip of his finger, loath to disturb his sleep. Then he brushed the same finger across her cheek over the top of his son's head and left it there.

His breath settled for the first time in days. He couldn't bear to part with either of them for tonight.

Tomorrow, he would keep himself at a distance, until he figured out how to make this ache a little more bearable. Tomorrow, he would ration himself on how much of his wife he could have.

The next evening, Mimi's steps slowed and she paused in the doorway, letting her gaze sweep slowly over the room. As if she were seeing it for the first time but really bracing herself for the sight that would meet her eyes.

The nursery was a haven of understated elegance—walls painted a soft dove gray accented with white crown molding. A pale blue mobile shaped like delicate Venetian gondolas hung above a polished white crib.

A tufted armchair sat in one corner, beside a bookshelf stocked with colorful storybooks she had started collecting long before Luca's birth. Warm, honey-colored wood floors gleamed faintly under the glow of a muted table lamp.

Near the large picture window that offered a glimpse of the shimmering Grand Canal, Renzo lay propped on his elbow on the thick wool rug. He had returned late last night, and she had stepped out of the penthouse before he had been awake, sticking to her own work schedule.

He was barefoot, the casual jeans and snug black sweater fitting him with effortless perfection. Two months into their marriage and her heart still stuttered at the sight of him—all that sexy masculinity sprawled around wherever she turned—as if it were all a dream.

His dark hair was slightly tousled, a stark contrast to his usual meticulously groomed appearance.

Luca, wrapped snugly in a soft knit blanket, blinked up at his father with wide, sleepy eyes. His hands, still so small and fragile, twitched slightly as if testing their strength. Renzo's deep voice was a soothing murmur, speaking Italian lullabies that melted the edges of Mimi's lingering tension.

He had been gone for only two days, and yet in the aftermath of bringing Luca home, she had realized how lonely she had been.

The wool rug was soft beneath her bare feet as she leaned against the doorframe, her chest painfully tight at the scene. If there were a picture of her heart beating outside of her, it would be this—the man she loved and their son together. "You two look comfortable," she said, infusing a teasing warmth she didn't feel into her words.

Renzo glanced up, his gaze instantly darkening as he swept it over her. She could live to be a hundred, but the thrill of his eyes landing on her would never pass. "You look...exhausted."

Mimi chuckled, stepping fully into the room and dropping onto her knees beside them. Instantly, a cocktail of scents greeted her nostrils—her son's baby powder and her husband's cologne. She felt dizzy, a rush of overwhelming love for both filling her. "I hate working out even as the trainer begins. It's only after that I feel the rush." She sighed and rubbed her face in Luca's belly. "It would be nice if we could feel the adrenaline rush before we do the hard things in life, wouldn't it? A little reminder that it would be worth it."

Renzo remained silent. She wondered if it was because he understood what she meant or if he didn't care. A hot prickle of tears greeted the backs of her eyes, and she blinked rapidly.

He had dragged her kicking and screaming into this marriage, given her a taste of how wonderful their relationship could be, and then distanced himself. She wanted to scream at him, demand he explain himself. Only he hadn't done anything to break the conditions of their agreement, had he?

It was she who had changed utterly. And even though it was her fault, she couldn't live with the unbearable ache of loving him and knowing he might never love her.

Lying down next to Luca, she grabbed his chubby hand and rubbed her nose in it. "What are you two talking about?"

Renzo shifted slightly, propping Luca up into his arms. Instantly, her son let out a long gurgle, excitement making his dark eyes shine.

God, he was tiny on that corded forearm, and yet Mimi never doubted that Renzo would temper his strength.

It was how he handled her too. Though she lived for the times when he lost control, when his raw need trumped his protective instincts and he let himself take what he needed from her. When he let her see how demanding he could be.

"I was telling him about Venice," he said. "How the city sounds different as it gets colder. You hear fewer boats at night and fewer footsteps on the bridges."

Mimi smiled, her gaze fixed on Luca. "Think he understood any of that?"

"Of course," Renzo said, not meeting her eyes. "He's very advanced for his age."

She laughed softly, this time brushing her fingers over Luca's feet. "I think he's just happy to be warm and fed. Aren't you, baby boy?"

Luca's mouth moved slightly, and Mimi swore his eyes lingered on hers for a moment longer than usual.

"I didn't realize what a big difference a few days makes in appearance," Renzo said, his tone tinged with awe. "Every day, I notice something new. Like how he looks at us now. Like he knows we're his."

Mimi's throat tightened as she glanced at her husband.

The light from the lamps caught on the sharp planes of his face, softening the usual intensity in his expression. There was something so tender, so unguarded, about the way he looked at Luca. And every time she caught that look, it made her realize that it was reserved only for their son.

No one else. But she wanted him to look at her like that too. She wanted so badly to be more than his son's mother, his sensible, competent wife or his lover when the mood struck. She wanted to be everything to him.

"I think he recognizes you already," she said, her voice soft.

Renzo chuckled, the rich sound filling the room. "He probably wonders why I talk so much."

Mimi smiled, shifting closer until their shoulders touched. The air between them felt warmer now, a subtle connection threading through the quiet moment.

But the warmth, the shared connection, would disappear the minute they were out of Luca's presence. And Mimi knew suddenly, despite wondering if she was shortchanging her son, that she couldn't bear to live like this anymore.

CHAPTER TWELVE

"What's this?" Mimi said a couple of hours later, staring at the official-looking envelope sitting on her pillow with her name scrawled on top.

It had taken them a long time to get Luca settled into his crib. She wondered if her own restlessness had triggered his crankiness.

The connecting door clicked behind Renzo. She turned to find him undoing the buttons on his shirt. Tension arced between them, sexual and otherwise.

He looked tired, with deep grooves settling under his eyes and around his mouth. In a moment, her frustration with him melted away.

She longed to go to him, to cradle his cheeks and brush her mouth against his, to feel his solid strength around her. She longed to offer him solace in whatever way she could.

But she wasn't sure if her efforts would be welcome, and that hurt immensely. She didn't know if he would welcome her admission of love either, or scoff at her for being such an easy fool. Nothing in her life had prepared her for facing him with that admission.

When he remained silent, she bristled. "Please don't tell me it's another gift."

"I had a lot of meetings with my lawyers this past

week, *cara*. It was convenient to take care of this too." His own frustration resonated in his words now. "And I don't get what is so strange about a husband arranging things for his wife. You're the one who calls them gifts."

With that parting shot, he went into the closet.

Mimi followed him, her patience dwindling with this cat and mouse game they were playing.

The colorful designer clothes hanging on her side of the closet, along with multiple boxes of expensive jewelry, brought her problem with him to the forefront. All the things Renzo insisted on buying for her, despite her protests.

She was Renzo DiCarlo's wife, as much as she didn't like to wear that as some kind of mantle. As such, there was always a certain amount of interest in her.

So yes, it made sense to upgrade her wardrobe and obtain some jewelry pieces and accessories.

She told herself that it was all part of a costume for a play she sometimes participated in. Especially since, whether she was dressed in designer duds or her usual black leggings and loose sweatshirts, the way he looked at her never changed.

It had begun with the equipment he had delivered to her, even before Luca had come home—expensive, state-of-the-art cameras and other accessories that she was afraid to even touch. Equipment that had made her drool like a child in a pastry shop.

She had refused at first, even though every inch of her had protested. And the rogue had persuaded her to keep it by kissing her, by telling her that if she was serious about her career, then she needed to invest in proper equipment.

Then had come the search for a house. An estate they

had finally found near Milan to Renzo's satisfaction—on the edge of Lake Como, to be precise—because Renzo insisted that at some point, Luca would need more space to play, and a sterile, monochromatic penthouse was the last place for a child.

And yet when his personal lawyer had come to have her sign some papers, Mimi had realized that the mansion had been deeded in her name. And another place in London, because her work might take her back to the city, and they needed a stable place for Luca.

Again, she had hotly protested. Again, he had convinced her that it made sense to have some properties in her name, that it was the wedding gift he had never given her. A place where they would build a bigger family, if they wanted to, at some point in the future.

The only thing that had stopped her from shouting that she wanted that with him was the flash of something in his eyes. And suddenly, she began to see the pattern.

Renzo bought her things—expensive houses and jewelry and video equipment.

Renzo was setting up properties for her, ostensibly, that were far away from where he would be most of the time, away from Venice, which was his main base.

Was he slowly trying to build a long-distance, perfectly polite marriage? Was he already bored with the domesticity Luca, and she, had forced on him?

For all that his family treated him as if he was an eternal fount granting their desires, he was only a man. There was no doubt that he was burnt out after Santo's death.

Did he resent her and Luca too, as being too needy, too dependent on him after all the responsibilities he had shouldered all his life?

The questions came at her fast, nearly knocking her off her feet.

She turned to demand he tell her the truth. And stilled.

He'd shrugged off his shirt, and the light from the overhead chandelier kissed every plane and ridge of his chest.

Even now, Mimi felt that near-manic urge to throw herself at him—to claw her fingers over that olive skin stretched taut over hard sinew, to lose herself in his rough, biting kiss, to urge him to bury himself inside her until all her doubts melted away.

Because when they were tangled up in each other's arms, there was no doubt that he wanted her in his life. That he wanted her. It was outside of the intimacy that she lost all her footing.

Now that she could see past her own misery, though, she noted the tension clamping his shoulders. "What's wrong? Is it Massimo? Is he in trouble again?"

A soft smile split his mouth. "No, apparently you were right about him. He apologized for being so...out of control in the last few months. He said he missed Santo. Neither of us realized that we should talk to each other about how much we miss our older brother."

"You have a thousand responsibilities to shoulder," she said, instantly coming to his defense. "What's his excuse?"

"You're a witch, *bella*. Because Massimo did have one." He unbuckled his trousers, pushed them off his tapered hips along with his boxer shorts. Utterly confident in his body. Utterly magnificent in his nakedness.

Then he pulled on gray sweatpants, and Mimi forced herself to focus. "Which is what?"

"Apparently, he has always been intimidated by me."

"Oh. That's not…impossible. You are a man with ruthless, exacting standards in every aspect of life, Renzo. Mere mortals could find it hard to please you."

"You've never failed, *bella*."

Mimi flushed, her skin nearly vibrating with the need to go to him. "By those exacting standards, you allow me a lot of leeway. And honestly, it's hard to read you, Renzo."

"Not for you," he retorted again.

"Again, only so much as you allow me," she said, busying herself with opening the new clothes she had ordered for Luca. "You very much control what I or anyone else perceives about you. You're a damned master at it."

She didn't care look at him, but she knew her words had landed. For a while, he didn't say anything. The expansive closet with its full-length mirrors and pristine marble floors suddenly felt too small and too cold to hold the tension crackling between them.

"So his not even trying to behave like a mature adult is valid because I have high standards?" Renzo sounded so aggravated by this, by her defense of Massimo, that Mimi stared at him. Something about his tone nagged at her, but she couldn't put her finger on it.

"No. I never said that. Massimo's good at trying to get out of a fix even when he's admitting that he's messed up. He's a charmer through and through. And honestly, with Santo so wrapped up in his own life and you buried in your business, I don't blame him for feeling lost."

"We should have had you there, refereeing our discussion."

This time, his disgruntlement was as clear as the cold draft of air kissing her skin. Mimi grabbed an old sweatshirt of Renzo's and pulled it on when he set that dark gaze on her.

"He pays attention to you," Renzo said. "I think he has a little crush on you."

Heat crept up her cheeks. "That's...ridiculous. We share some interests. As much as you mock him, I think he's serious about photography. You wanted him to change, Renzo. Give him a chance now."

Gaze thoughtful, Renzo nodded.

"What about Chiara?" she said, knowing he needed to talk about his family. Only then could she address their own relationship. "Your mother has been visiting regularly, but she doesn't mention Chiara. And neither do I," Mimi admitted, suddenly feeling guilty. "I mean, I know I should try to make amends with her, but with Luca coming home and everything else, it's just been a lot, and I..."

Renzo took her hands in his and squeezed. When Mimi thought he would pull her to him and wrap those strong arms around her—her entire being nearly ready to fling herself at him—he let go.

Hurt crashed through her, and suddenly it felt unbearable. Why did he touch her only in a sexual context? What happened to the Renzo who had teased her, made fun of her and provoked her? Why was he spending so much time away from her and Luca when he was the one who insisted on this marriage?

Had it all been to control the situation and her?

"I haven't spoken to her either. I did pay off her husband's debt, in case you thought I acted on my threat. Mama said they might be filing for divorce. Chiara has made her bed, though, and she needs to make a decision—whether she wants to lie in it or not."

He paused and then raised a hand as if to stop her next question. Something like resignation settled into his stark features. "I've given up trying to manage their lives. If they get in trouble, I will help. But no more expectations that they will behave, that they will fix their mistakes, or that they will understand me."

Mimi's heart ached for him as she followed him to their bedroom. And then her gaze fell on the damned envelope again.

"Open it," he said with that arrogant tilt of his head that she had come to recognize as a tell of his uncertainty.

She almost protested, but the last thing she wanted to spend her energy on was a silly fight.

Mimi opened the envelope and quickly skimmed the documents. It was a lot of legalese, but she understood enough to feel as if she had been burned. She dropped them onto the bed, anger sparking and lighting up her flashpoint.

"What the hell? Why are you settling this much money on me?" She scoffed at her incapability to do mental math. "I can't even convert that number into pounds. I didn't ask you for any of this."

"You're overreacting."

Mimi was so angry at this statement that she simply sputtered at him.

"You know I set up trust funds for Chiara's children, for Massimo. I did one for Luca, and this is for you."

"Why? Are you planning to divorce me soon? Are you worried that I might ask for too much?"

"Of course not. You are the one who made up the one-year plan, not me."

Mimi folded her hands and glared at him. "Did no one

tell you that the last thing you should say to your wife is that she's overreacting?"

"You do overreact when it comes to me buying you anything. We've been through this, Mimi. I am a rich man. I like to buy my wife certain things. One would think you'd learn to accept them with grace."

"Not when it feels like you're buying me out for some reason, Renzo. I told you when you proposed this whole arrangement—" she still couldn't bring herself to say *this marriage* "—that I don't want anything from you. Except your support in raising Luca when we separate."

He remained stubbornly mute.

"So, are we separating? Is that what you want? All these new residences you have been buying me in different cities, these overnight trips you take, the way you're never here to—"

"I never what? You're telling me I'm failing in my duty as a husband and a father?"

Duty...there was that word again.

She had never hated a word in the language so much as she did then. And it also gave her the answer for the questions that plagued her day and night like vultures pecking at her tender flesh.

She would always be another responsibility to him, nothing more. Another burden he had taken on. And maybe because she was a novelty to him right now, or because she provided easy, convenient, hassle-free relief in the form of sex, he gave her and demanded physical intimacy.

But how long would that last if he saw her as another item on his to-do list? How long would it last if they had nothing else outside it?

As hard as she fought, a tear slipped down her cheek. Because she didn't understand how to get back what they had once had. She didn't even know if it had been anything more than a mirage of a connection brought on by their shared grief for their lost siblings and love for the innocent life they were bringing into the world.

"I want to go to London for Christmas and take Luca with me," she blurted out, having reached the end of her tether.

His head jerked up as if someone had punched him. And he continued to stare at her for several long moments without a question or a statement.

Mimi wrapped her arms around herself and looked out the large window. The world outside seemed to be going on at its usual rhythms while hers...was tilting upside down. "One of the documentaries I made when I was pregnant—about prenatal healthcare for women from lower economic backgrounds—got nominated for an award. The banquet is a few days before Christmas, in London. I want to—I have to attend. And I want to bring Luca with me. There's a bunch of friends who want to see him, and I...need a break."

"A break from what?" Renzo finally said.

"From being cooped up here," she said, meeting his eyes.

Please, ask me not to leave, her foolish heart murmured. *Ask me to stay. Tell me you'll fix whatever's gone wrong between us.*

The lines of strain around his mouth deepened as he regarded her. "How long are you talking about?"

"I don't know. I think you have a lot to deal with right now, with that new resort being built. And I need to go back to my life for a little while." She bit her lip, arresting the bitterness that wanted to spew forth. "Luca's the most important thing in my life now, and...there are things I need to sort out with my mother too. I've been running away from my own home for too long."

"And you're not now?" he demanded, his question sharp as a knife. But he didn't give her a chance to respond. "Whatever you want, *bella*. Just do me the favor of staying at the London flat I bought you recently." His mouth twisted wryly. "Seems like I have foresight."

And then he walked out.

No arguments. No threats. No discussion.

Leaving Mimi alone with their son.

CHAPTER THIRTEEN

THE SLEEK BLACK chauffeur-driven Bentley pulled up to the entrance of the Mayfair Grand DiCarlo, its golden lights spilling onto the rain-slicked pavement. London glowed, festive and alive, twinkling in the drizzle.

Inside the car, Mimi sat frozen, her fingers curled around the cold glass of her award.

She had won.

Best Documentary.

She should have been elated. She should have been riding the high of the applause, the champagne toasts, the congratulations. And yet all she could think about was *him*.

The moment they announced her name, the small banquet hall had erupted.

Thunderous waves of applause had rolled over her, shaking the air, stealing her breath. Strangers had stood for her. Her peers and friends and her parents had cheered.

It was a small achievement in a small career, but she was proud of herself. Because her best work had come when she had persevered through the roughest year of her life.

And yet she wasn't…happy.

She felt as if she were bodily present but absent in

spirit, as if she were playacting in someone else's life. It had been the same in the last week since she had left Venice.

Because the only person she had wanted to share her achievement and her joy with wasn't there.

Renzo wasn't there.

It had been his voice in her ear in those fractious weeks when Luca was still at the hospital. Asking her to tell him about her latest project. Then, low and certain, urging her to apply for the award when she'd nearly talked herself out of it. When she'd sat at her laptop, doubting every word of the essay she'd written for the application, wondering if the documentary she'd worked on during her pregnancy was too bleak, it had been his belief in her passion that had made her press Send.

You're not just talented, cara, *but hold a unique perspective. Let the world see it.*

She had ached to turn to him, to see his face in the crowd, to rush into his arms and hear that deep, gravelly voice in her ear again. To hear him call her his clever, competent, sexy-as-sin wife again. To see the glimmer of pride in his eyes.

But he hadn't been there.

And in the days since she had left, he hadn't called her even once. Their nanny made sure he chatted with Luca every morning and evening.

Her chest twisted in a tight, painful knot when she heard the deep lilt of his Italian as he greeted their son. Her soul ached to lay eyes on him. She had resisted.

And yet when she'd accepted the award and looked into the glare of flashbulbs and cameras in the crowd, for just a second, she'd thought she'd seen him.

Tall, unmistakably handsome, watching her with that quiet, unreadable intensity that always made her pulse skitter.

She had felt it in how her nape prickled, how her body sang. She had felt him close.

But when she had stepped off the stage, searching, there had been no sign of him. Of course, Renzo wasn't there.

It was just another trick of her own foolish mind, another cruel mirage her hopeless love offered to soothe her.

God, she was going mad. Seeing him in places he wasn't, hearing his voice in echoes that didn't exist.

The driver cleared his throat, and she realized the car had stopped.

Right. The hotel.

Tomorrow was Christmas Eve. And while every inch of her wanted to hide under a weighted blanket and not emerge until the New Year's, this was her son's first Christmas.

She owed it to him, and herself, to celebrate their togetherness, to start new traditions. She had lost too much recently to not see what she did have. Even if her heart felt like it was dented in a hundred places.

The air was crisp, carrying the scent of damp pavement and expensive perfume. Heels clicking against the marble, she stepped into the grand lobby, only to come to a sudden standstill. Her breath danced in her throat, almost choking her.

Was that Massimo stepping out of the grand elevator? Or was her mind creating mirages again?

With that long-limbed stride and easy laughter, his

gaze caught on the phone in his hand, he strolled out the other exit, utterly at ease.

If he was here, why hadn't he contacted her? Why was he in London at all? It wasn't as though their mother would let him out of her sight during the holiday season. Only Renzo could convince her to let him travel with him...

The realization hit her like a blow to the chest.

That meant Renzo was here in London. It *was* her husband she'd seen at the awards ceremony. He had been present in the audience, hiding in the shadows, but hadn't shown himself.

How dare he hide away like a thief? How dare he play with her feelings?

A host of emotions crashed over her, all hot and sharp and unbearable.

Anger. Longing. Heartbreak.

Anger won out, propelling her forward. Her pulse thundered as she pivoted toward the front desk, jaw tight.

"Hi, I have a question," she said, voice sharp.

The receptionist barely looked up before reaching under the counter. "Good evening, Mrs. DiCarlo. Did you need a new key card?" His voice was smooth, professional, with the polite indifference of someone who dealt with VIPs daily. He simply slid a key card across the marble counter as if this was routine.

Mimi's breath caught.

Mrs. DiCarlo.

Because the poor man assumed that she would know her goddamned husband was already here. At his own hotel.

Her hands trembled as she took the smooth white keycard, her blood boiling now.

The private elevator ride felt both too slow and too fast. Matching the uneven rhythm of her own heartbeats.

She pushed it open, stepping into the darkened expanse. The only light came from the city skyline, gleaming through the floor-to-ceiling windows. The room smelled clean, expensive, undeniably like her arrogant, suave Italian husband.

Her pulse went haywire as she finally spotted him.

Standing by the window, jacket discarded, sleeves rolled up, a glass of whiskey in his hand. He didn't seem surprised that she was standing there.

"You were at the gala, weren't you?" she demanded without preamble.

"Buonasera, cara."

The whiskey-deep timbre of his voice made her knees shake. "Answer my question, Renzo."

"Yes, I was there." He didn't turn to look at her, though. Instead, he swirled the amber liquid in his glass, exhaling slowly. As if he couldn't bear to meet her eyes. "Congratulations, *bella*. You were glowing up there. That quick speech you gave...everyone could hear your passion for what you do."

"What the hell kind of a game are you playing, Renzo? How long have you been in London?" Her voice cracked with betrayal. "You're toying with me, with my feelings."

Finally, he looked at her. His dark eyes were unreadable, and tension radiated from him. "I didn't mean to hurt you. Not today, not before."

She took a step closer, her heart slamming against her ribs. "So what? You were spying on me?"

"For what reason?" A flash of anger broke through the surface.

Mimi welcomed it. She hated it when he looked...tired. Or burnt out. Or as if he was losing a battle. Which was exactly how he had looked that night in their bedroom.

Ten odd days of distance from him, from her own confused thoughts, gave her crystal-clear clarity. There had been a kind of resignation when he talked about his family, but there had been acceptance too. Like setting down a burden that he had carried for so long. So, his unhappiness had been because of her? Because of where they stood with each other?

Should she have had more patience, more courage and faith in their relationship? In him and herself?

He'd even taunted that she was running away again. But she hadn't paid attention, miserable in her love for him. How had she not even told him? How had she failed herself without even trying?

"I didn't want to ruin your moment," he said, bringing her to the present. "I didn't want to make it about us."

"Ruin it?" Her voice broke. And her self-control lay in shreds at her feet, knowing that it was her own fault for not verbalizing what she needed from him. For failing him and herself both. "Renzo, you being there was the only thing that would have made it feel real."

A muscle ticked in his jaw, but he said nothing.

She swallowed hard. "Why did you come? Why not tell me that you're here? Why..."

His eyes flickered, something raw passing through them. The intensity of it stole her anger and her words. "Because I'm a coward who's still trying to figure out how to tell you that I'm in love with you, *bella*."

The breath whooshed from her lungs, and she swayed on her feet, the entire day catching up with her.

Renzo set his glass down with a thud and caught her.

Renzo kicked the door of the bedroom shut behind him with a kick. Not that anyone from the staff would dare disturb them. But with Massimo around, he didn't want to take any chances.

He gently deposited Mimi on the bed and sat down by her side.

Like a prickly cat, she pushed away from his hold and scooted up to sit against the tufted headboard. The hem of the pink silk dress she wore bunched up against her knees and higher, exposing long, smooth limbs to his greedy eyes. The sweetheart neckline fought against the heaving thrust of her breasts, revealing the upper swells.

He gritted his teeth—it was hardly the time for him to drool over her—and met her gaze.

Color dusted her cheeks. Her hair, smooth and silky like a rainfall in the pitch-black of the night, danced around her bare shoulders. She looked…so beautiful that it was an ache to look at her and not touch her.

"Did you…" she licked her lower lip nervously "…say what I thought I heard?"

He nodded.

Tears filled her big brown eyes, overflowing instantly. "You're not playing with me?"

It cleaved him to see her so hurt, so disbelieving. "I've never said anything to you that I didn't mean, *bella*."

"But all those gifts…"

A self-deprecating laugh escaped him. "After that party, I realized I was already falling for you. Seeing

Rosa…" he thrust a hand through his hair "…made me realize you were the only person in my life who didn't want my power or wealth or influence. I had nothing you could possibly want. So I decided, with my twisted logic, that I would drown you in so many lavish things that you would see the value of having me in your life."

"That *is* twisted," she said, honest to the last. "I wouldn't have minded those…gifts so much if you hadn't retreated from me. One minute, you're engraving yourself into my flesh, my heart, and the next, you're treating me as if I'm another burden you couldn't escape. You stopped teasing me, provoking me, touching me… I felt desolate."

"Not touch you?" Renzo said, shaking his head. "I couldn't keep my hands off you."

"Sex is not the only intimacy we shared. In fact, it was the last thing that fell into place. The grand finish that told me how perfect you are. But suddenly, outside of sex, you didn't…touch me at all. Here I was, sitting with the realization that I was in love with you, and you couldn't bear to look at me."

Renzo stilled. Every inch of his body pulled toward hers as if she were using her very own gravity on him. "You love me?"

She swiped at her tears with the backs of her hands. "It feels like forever already."

"Why didn't you tell me?" Even he could hear the awe in his tone.

"You know my mother and I have issues, right?"

He laughed at her dry tone.

"I know that your family and mine always seems to be front and center of our lives, but this is the last time I bring her or Pia up, I promise."

He took her hand in his and traced the knuckles gently. "I'll listen to whatever you tell me, *bella*. Especially if it means it will remove the shadows from your eyes."

"I...she raised me when she was single, and my deadbeat father had already fled. But she wasn't...the maternal sort. She loved her acting career the most, and I..." She swallowed and looked at her hands in her lap. "Even as a child, I hated being the center of attention. She wasn't cruel or negligent, Renzo. She was just...not overtly loving."

Renzo grabbed her tightly clasped hands and kissed each knuckle. "Stop excusing her behavior toward you, *bella*."

"I'm not. The last week I spent with her, I reexamined it all. With the perspective of an adult and as a new mother myself. She had no support of any kind, and she did her best. We would have muddled through somehow..."

"Except she married John, and Pia came into your lives."

Mimi laughed. The tip of her nose was red, and her eyes were still damp, but she was the most beautiful sight he had ever seen. "Pia..." she whispered and sighed. "I adored her from the beginning, you know. She was everything I wasn't. Beautiful, bright, witty...and petty and manipulative as hell."

Renzo laughed too.

"She and Mom got along like a house on fire from day one. I didn't mind it one bit. John was lovely and kind to me. Until Pia told me that he was her father and not mine, and she wasn't going to let me steal him from her. And yet I never doubted that she loved me too. She was the one who bought me my first camera, did you know?"

Renzo shook his head.

Mimi smiled. "I...see now that for all that she was, she was also very insecure. It made her needy and manipulative. She wanted Mom and John and even me all to herself. We weren't supposed to want or love each other or anyone else. But I didn't understand it as a teenager. When I..." her throat bobbed "...found her kissing my boyfriend, my best friend of years... I lost faith in myself. And yet I'm not sure if I would have believed her if she had told me that he had been hitting on her for a long while. She made me see the truth even though it broke my heart in the process."

"You're making her out to be better than she was, Mimi."

"No, I'm seeing her clearly for the first time. I'm seeing her not as this girl I desperately wanted to please and love, but as a whole person. I needed to sort this all out in my head, for myself, for Luca. I needed to realize that she loved me in her own way, and I loved her. Because one day, far into the future, I want to tell him about her and Santo. They deserved to be known to him, don't you think?"

His own eyes damp, Renzo nodded. How expansive and strong his fragile wife's heart was, and he had tried to buy his way into it.

"I had to see the past clearly for the last time, see how she and Mom shaped me, so that I can be free. And you...tasting what life could be like with you gave me the courage."

"Free for what, *bella*?"

"To dare to want you for myself, Renzo." Fresh tears drew tracks over her cheeks. "To have the courage to tell you that I fell in love with you, despite my every effort to resist you. I love you so much that it's like carrying around an ache. To trust in myself and you, enough to know that after helping me see myself in this new way, you love me too."

Nothing in the world would have stopped him then. Renzo climbed into the bed and pulled her to him.

Their kiss was salty and swift and clunky but *Cristo*, he didn't want to live another moment without tasting her. Without holding her.

He pressed her back into the bed and let her feel his weight, his need for her. He trailed frenzied kisses over her forehead, her eyes, her temples, her cheeks, and finally he found her lips again.

This time their kiss was soft, slow, even as her hands wandered restlessly over his back. "I love you, *cara mia*. With all my faulty heart. The idea of you leaving me at some vague point in the future twisted me out of my head. I…distanced myself from you because I knew I was failing. And all along, all I had to do was tell you that I love you."

"Please, never do that to me again. Never pull away after you've shown me what love can be, how colorful and happy I can be with you."

Renzo pressed their foreheads together, his own breath shallow now. "Never again, *bella*. You're mine. Your smart brain, your tart mouth, your curvy body, your generous heart, your sparkling soul…you are all mine, Mimi. And I'm never letting you out of my sight ever again."

It was a while later—although not too long, since Renzo had been in frenzied need—that they went to collect their son from John and her mother.

Legs thrown into his lap in the back seat of the Bentley, Mimi clung to her husband as he talked about how they would return to Venice that very night and celebrate Christmas by themselves.

No one was allowed to interrupt them, he decided.

"Maybe just Massimo?" she asked, knowing how attached her son was becoming to his uncle.

Renzo growled that he would not share her with anyone, not even his charming brother.

Mimi called him a jealous, overbearing brute, and he kissed her.

And she decided she didn't care how Renzo acted as long as he kissed her and held her and loved her like he did.

Like she was the sun, and the stars, and the sky all combined.

* * * * *

Were you blown away by the drama in
*Baby Before Vows? Then why not explore
these other dazzling stories by Tara Pammi!*

Fiancée for the Cameras
Contractually Wed
Her Twin Secret
Vows to a King
His Forgotten Wife

Available now!

Get up to 4 Free Books!

We'll send you 2 free books from each series you try PLUS a free Mystery Gift.

FREE Value Over $25

Both the **Harlequin Presents** and **Harlequin Medical Romance** series feature exciting stories of passion and drama.

YES! Please send me 2 FREE novels from Harlequin Presents or Harlequin Medical Romance and my FREE gift (gift is worth about $10 retail). After receiving them, if I don't wish to receive any more books, I can return the shipping statement marked "cancel." If I don't cancel, I will receive 6 brand-new larger-print novels every month and be billed just $7.19 each in the U.S., or $7.99 each in Canada, or 4 brand-new Harlequin Medical Romance Larger-Print books every month and be billed just $7.19 each in the U.S. or $7.99 each in Canada, a savings of 20% off the cover price. It's quite a bargain! Shipping and handling is just 50¢ per book in the U.S. and $1.25 per book in Canada.* I understand that accepting the 2 free books and gift places me under no obligation to buy anything. I can always return a shipment and cancel at any time. The free books and gift are mine to keep no matter what I decide.

Choose one:
- ☐ **Harlequin Presents Larger-Print** (176/376 BPA G36Y)
- ☐ **Harlequin Medical Romance** (171/371 BPA G36Y)
- ☐ **Or Try Both!** (176/376 & 171/371 BPA G36Z)

Name (please print)

Address   Apt. #

City   State/Province   Zip/Postal Code

Email: Please check this box ☐ if you would like to receive newsletters and promotional emails from Harlequin Enterprises ULC and its affiliates. You can unsubscribe anytime.

Mail to the Harlequin Reader Service:
IN U.S.A.: P.O. Box 1341, Buffalo, NY 14240-8531
IN CANADA: P.O. Box 603, Fort Erie, Ontario L2A 5X3

Want to explore our other series or interested in ebooks? Visit www.ReaderService.com or call 1-800-873-8635.

---

*Terms and prices subject to change without notice. Prices do not include sales taxes, which will be charged (if applicable) based on your state or country of residence. Canadian residents will be charged applicable taxes. Offer not valid in Quebec. This offer is limited to one order per household. Books received may not be as shown. Not valid for current subscribers to the Harlequin Presents or Harlequin Medical Romance series. All orders subject to approval. Credit or debit balances in a customer's account(s) may be offset by any other outstanding balance owed by or to the customer. Please allow 4 to 6 weeks for delivery. Offer available while quantities last.

Your Privacy—Your information is being collected by Harlequin Enterprises ULC, operating as Harlequin Reader Service. For a complete summary of the information we collect, how we use this information and to whom it is disclosed, please visit our privacy notice located at https://corporate.harlequin.com/privacy-notice. Notice to California Residents – Under California law, you have specific rights to control and access your data. For more information on these rights and how to exercise them, visit https://corporate.harlequin.com/california-privacy. For additional information for residents of other U.S. states that provide their residents with certain rights with respect to personal data, visit https://corporate.harlequin.com/other-state-residents-privacy-rights/.

HPHM25